The Lynching
Of Hiram Wilson

Chariton, Iowa 1870

A Novel

by

Buzz Malone

Published by Buzz Malone Books

A Createspace Production

Cover Photography by Lorri Forst

Other Books by This Author
Available On Amazon.com

The Ghosts of Melrose

The Lynching of Hiram Wilson by Buzz Malone

Dedications

I would like to dedicate *The Lynching of Hiram Wilson* to my own three sons; Tony, Jesse, and Mason. If there is anything good about me as a person, it is because of them. I could not be any prouder than I am of my sons and the young men they are each becoming. Boys, this one's for you!

Also, I would like to recognize my better half, Lorri. Without her continued guidance, support, and "constructive" criticism, none of these stories would have ever been shared with the world. She believed in me more than I have ever believed in myself. It is her who pushes me through every word and every chapter until the book is complete.

I would also like to mention that Lorri worked countless hours on *The Ghosts of Melrose,* editing and proof reading it to perfection. Then, after she did all of that, I still managed to submit the wrong version of the book for publication; hence the typos that still exist.

Finally, I would like to thank the people of Southern Iowa. These are truly YOUR stories and I thank you for allowing me to share them with the rest of the world.

Introduction

This, my second novel in what I have come to personally refer to as the *Lucas County Chronicles* is completely unrelated to *The Ghosts of Melrose*. However, like *Ghosts,* and like most good stories, this book began with a true, but mostly forgotten tale. The account that it opens with *is* a genuine account from the annals of Lucas County, Iowa history. It is part of an actual newspaper story from the day.

What I thought was most compelling however, is what the newspaper story doesn't say. What stories were involved in leading up to the infamous article that has been buried in the sands of time and lost from the collective memory of the community? Sadly, we will never really know of course, but like archeologists digging for the emotional truth behind a handful of facts, we as people are drawn collectively to the human elements behind the news stories. We want to know who they were and why they did the things they did.

To that end, and to creatively speculate on real historical events, I give to you the novel, *The Lynching of Hiram Wilson.*

While the opening account is true and I have retained the names of the main players (Hiram Wilson and Gaylord Lyman), everything in the novel portion is creative, fictitious speculation and conjecture. The activities, thoughts, and words of the characters contained herein are mere fantasies of the author's overactive imagination.

I hope you enjoy the story as much I have enjoyed the telling of it.

Chapter 1   The Aftermath

Chariton, Iowa July 1870

From the Chariton Democrat of July 12, 1870:

Last Wednesday was a day of terrible excitement in Chariton, and one that will long be remembered. It was fruitful in crime, and speedy in retribution. Sheriff Lyman was murdered in cold blood upon one of the public streets, by a horse-thief, and the murderer expiated his double crime at the end of a rope. We herewith give a full statement of the melancholy events.

Early on Wednesday morning a young man arrived in town, having in his possession a horse, and his efforts to sell it aroused the suspicion of some of our citizens that he had stolen it. He finally sold the horse to Capt. W. I. Robison, for $50 and a watch. Sheriff Lyman, becoming confirmed in his suspicions, took the fellow in charge, while he was at a saloon just south of the southeast corner of the square. The prisoner insisted *that he was innocent, said that he lived near Freedom, in this county, and could bring men to testify as to his good character. The names that he gave were those of persons unknown to the sheriff or any others who heard them, and they told him so. He then wanted to go alone and bring persons who, he said, would vouch for him. The sheriff was willing that he should go, but that he should also go with him. To this the thief objected, and moved off a few steps as if about to walk off alone. The sheriff told him to "hold on," and also started as if to follow him. The young man stopped, turned around, pulled out a large navy revolver, and told the sheriff to stop --- that if he did not, he would shoot him. Sheriff Lyman was himself unarmed, but he hardly believed that the man would shoot, and deliberately made another step or two toward him --- when the fearful report of the pistol in the man's hands showed that he was as desperate as he pretended to be. The sheriff threw up his hands, and exclaiming, "Oh Lord! He has killed me," fell forward upon the sidewalk.*

The murderer at once started upon a run, and turning around the corner of Dennis & Kittredge's wagon factory, made for the alley running east, closely followed by one or two men. Reaching a farmer's horse that was tied in the alley, he was cutting it loose as his pursuers came nearly up with him. He pointed his pistol at the foremost one in such a manner as to cause them to stop a moment, when he jumped upon the horse, and broke for the timber, about half a mile east of town, known as Baker's grove. Reaching the fence that encloses the timber, he dismounted, left the horse, and sight of him was lost. The alarm was speedily raised, and the whole town turned out. Those who could raise weapons armed themselves, and all who could procure horses followed after him as fast as their horses could carry them, two or three hundred others followed on foot. The shooting took place at half past eleven o'clock and by one o'clock nearly three hundred persons were in and around the grove hunting him. The search continued for three or four hours, but as no system has as yet been established, it promised to be fruitless and many of those who had missed their dinners began to wend their way homeward.

About four o'clock, however, organization was secured, and the company started through the brush from south to north, in regular picket line, men being also stationed at regular distances to watch for the game. Mr. Copeland, the banker, was the first man to discover him, and while he started to find assistance and direct others how two proceed, two young men --- mere boys --- named Thomas Martin and Solomon Dawson, came upon him --- neither party seeing the other until they had come within five or six feet of each other. The thief and murderer was coming toward them in a stooping attitude, with his pistol pointed at Martin, and demanded of him in a sharp whisper to "keep still." Martin made for him, and when the man saw there could be no escape without a fight, he fired at Martin, the shot passing over his shoulder. With that, Martin struck him over the head with his gun, partially stunning him and almost knocking him down. He then sprang upon the desperado, threw him down, and in a moment more assistance had come, when the villain surrendered.

He was immediately pinioned, and brought to town, his captors having hold of each arm. He came very near being lynched in the woods, but a statement to the effect that Sheriff Lyman desired to see him, was all that saved him then. When the crowd arrived in town, the excitement reached a high pitch, and he would probably have been hung the moment he reached the square, had not another request come from the sheriff for permission to see his murderer. A small party took the prisoner in charge, and conducted him to the sheriff, who recognized him. The fellow told the sheriff that he was the man who had shot him, that he was sorry for it, and asked his forgiveness. Lyman unhesitatingly expressed his forgiveness, and the murderer was taken back toward the court house.

At this juncture, a man appeared with a new rope in his hand and raised the cry of "hang him!" "hang him!" and then such an excitement occurred as but few men ever before witnessed. Some well-disposed citizens interfered, and counseled respect for the laws, and asked that the culprit be given a chance for his life, or at least a fair trial by jury; and with great efforts the mass of the crowd was kept back, and the prisoner was fairly whirled into a small room in the court house, and the door closed.

The feeling of the crowd seemed to subside, and by six o'clock hopes were freely expressed that the people would let the law have its proper course. This, though advocated by a majority of the well-disposed citizens of the community, was strongly opposed by others, and there seemed to be a determination on their part that the murder should not escape. They maintained that it looked like imbecility to spend time and money to punish this man, as all knew he ought to be punished, and there were those who would not depart until the ends of justice should be satisfied. The terrible news becoming spread through the country, the "vigilantes" or anti-horse thief society, begun to put in an appearance, each one seeming to understand the situation, and evincing great coolness and determination. At half past ten o'clock, it was announced that Gaylord Lyman, the victim, had breathed his last, and then the doom of his murderer was sealed. A crowd was at the court house, a rope had been procured, and a formal demand for the prisoner was made by the captain of the vigilantes. The officers, of course, refused to deliver him up, but about that time two heavy beams came against the door, and the prisoner was soon at the mercy of an outraged community. He was taken to the south door of the court house, and the rope being adjusted about his neck, and the other end being passed in at a window upstairs, he was asked if he had anything to say, and here is his reply:

'Gentlemen --- I want you all to forgive me; I am a poor boy; my mother died when I was small. It is the first time I ever committed a crime; I was in liquor at the time.'

Further remarks were cut short by a severe tightening of the rope, and Hiram Wilson, a confessed horse-thief and murderer, had severed his earthly connection. Hiram Wilson is the name that he gave. He said that his father's home was in Putnam County, Missouri, about five miles from Warsaw, in Wayne county. He was twenty-one years old, sandy complexion, red hair, shock headed, five feet eight inches high, and would weigh about 155 pounds. He had a bad look, apparently brutalized in all his nature, and betrayed but little anxiety for his situation until the final demand was made upon the officers, when he begged of them to save him, and on being told that his time had come, he pleaded to have his shackles taken off, and that was all he asked. He was a desperate character, and would have fought like a tiger. He met his fate as he would a dinner or an ordinary business matter, and seemed, to the last, to feel that he was still worth several dead men. When the church-bell commenced tolling for Lyman, Wilson had "passed in his checks," and was shortly after cut down, life having been pronounced extinct. His body was taken into the court house, where it remained until Thursday morning, when, an inquest having been held, he was taken by *the sexton and buried in the "Potter's Field" (now called Douglass Cemetery: FDM), and his relations were notified of what had taken place. The statement of Wilson that he was in liquor when he did the shooting, was wholly untrue, and no one who saw the deliberation and coolness with which he committed the deed, and his activity in escaping, will believe that he had been drinking to excess.*

Perhaps we should have stated earlier that the sheriff, immediately after being shot, was taken into Uncle Billy Lewis's house, when medical aid was at once called. Doctors Gibbon, Stutsman and Heed did all that could be done to relieve his sufferings, but they knew that his life must be brief. The ball entered his right spine (side?), about the third or fourth rib, penetrating his lung, and lodging somewhere near the spine. He lived just eleven hours after receiving the wound. The deceased leaves a family of three children, and a wife, whose death has been hourly looked for several days past. He was in limited circumstances, which will make the sad occurrence still more painful to the bereaved family, which so much needed his fatherly support.

The sad occurrence spread its gloom over the entire community, and while there may be a few who do not endorse the means by which justice was administered to the criminal, yet there is not a man who can say that he did not deserve all that he got. In moment ol sober reflection there is not a community in the land where it would be more difficult to raise a mob than in Chariton, and we do not believe that when the facts in the case go out into the world, there will be many who will censure us for what, under other circumstances, might be looked upon as lawlessness. The necessity for such summary measures is to be regretted, but there are cases where statute laws fail to accomplish their object, and our citizens were deter-

mined that this should not prove an instance of that kind. And while they well knew that the crime deserved the punishment visited upon by the culprit, they also thought best to make an example of him, in the hope that it might have salutary effect, and secure us from such high-handed outrages in the future.

While we write, the funeral of the sheriff takes place. A gloomy sadness is visible upon every countenance. Business is suspended, the work-shops are closed, and people of all classes have turned out en masse, to accompany the remains to their last resting place. The Odd Fellows and other societies are out in full strength, and the quietness and earnestness of the demonstration, would be sufficient to convince any one that the tragic termination of Sheriff Lyman's life is regarded as a calamity upon the community. He was respected and liked by all who knew him, and if there were any who ever conceived an unkind feeling for him, that feeling gave place to real sorrow at his death.

There were many exciting and ludicrous incidents connected with the tragedy and the chase. Old Joe Johnson was one of the first to follow the murderer, and when he was about to jump upon the horse, "old Joe" came rather close to him. Wilson pointed the pistol at him and told him to get back, and (back) he got. John Reed was the first to arm himself, and could have shot Wilson, had not some women and children, who had been called to the street by the excitement, been in range of his gun. Capt. Leeman was the first to follow him on horse, and they had an exciting race to the timber --- Leeman being not more than twenty steps behind him when he ran into the bush, and had he been armed, he could easily have shot him. But he saw where Wilson ran into the bushes, and discovered the direction he had taken, which aided greatly in the capture. During the hunt in the woods, Wilson at one time, fell in with the line and pretended to join the search. Squire Gallagher thought he recognized him as being the man they were after, and asked him where he came from, who he was, etc.

After the prisoner was brought to town, he pointed out Ed Lewis and said that fellow would have ridden over him once, while he was in the weeds had he not drawn up his feet. Jesse Coles was also so close to Wilson at one time that the latter was on the point of shooting him and taking his horse, and would have done so had he not just then heard other voices near at hand. By a statement heretofore published, an impression was created that the marshal brought the fellow into town. Such is not the fact. The marshal was in town when the news came that Wilson had been arrested, and he then took a horse and went out and met the party that had him in charge, just as they reached the outskirts of town, when he assumed the direction of their movements; but he had no more to do with it than anybody else had. Martin and Dawson kept their hold upon the prisoner until they reached the square. Among those who were most clamorous for the hanging of Wilson, we noticed a Methodist preacher and while we can easily account for his feelings upon the subject, we cannot see how he will be able to reconcile his acts with his professions of love and mercy for the unfortunate. Another preacher, we are told, was quite officious at the hanging, and was the first to approach the hanging man, and feeling his pulse, pronounced life extinct. He probably looked upon it as a work of love and mercy. 2We might go on indefinitely with the mention of similar circumstances, but we believe that in giving the foregoing report, we have done our duty to the public."

From the Burlington Hawkeye Newspaper:

The shocking tragedy at Chariton on Wednesday adds another to the too numerous list that already makes up a dark page in the history of our state. The crime leading to the summary execution of the murderer was very unprovoked and aggravating. A quite, inoffensive law abiding citizen, and an officer of the law in the proper discharge of his duty, was suddenly shot down by a horse thief whom he had arrested, and in a few hours expired. His family of little children left fatherless, and his wife almost a maniac, and even threatened with death on account of her sudden and overwhelming grief. The perpetrator, a miserable outlaw from Missouri and doubtless a member of one of those gangs of horse thieves and cut throats who have long infested southwestern Iowa, and whose conviction, even after arrest, has been almost impossible on account of their strong organizations and accomplices in almost every county.

Under the circumstances we are not surprised that summary vengeance was taken on this guilty wretch. The provocation was very great. Still we can but deeply regret that the citizens there could not have saved their community and the state from the reproach which attaches to every case of summary vengeance. If there was a case of justifiable lynching in Iowa, this was probably one. And yet with all our knowledge of the circumstances and sympathy with the cruelly bereaved family of Sheriff Ly man, the certainty of the criminal's guilt, and the long series of outrages of which this was the culmination, we cannot approve or even excuse the conduct of those who hurried the murderer into eternity without judge or jury.

Chapter 2   Six Months Earlier

January 12, 1870

Gaylord Lyman sprang abruptly upright in his bed with a start. Sweat poured down his forehead and he wiped it away with his shirt sleeve. He'd been dreaming about them again. It had been years since it happened, but still they came to him at night while he slept.

Over ten years had passed since he'd been in that detail. Most times, he could just sort of forget about it. But every once in a while, when he least expected it, the Nebraska Territory would come flooding back in to the front of his mind like a burst dam. Sometimes it would happen all of a sudden like with the sound of a bird chirping or the smell of horse blood. Other times they came in his sleep, sneaking up on him when he wasn't ready and he was least able to stop it; just like they had done to him that night while he slept; just like they had done to all of them that night over a decade before. It was always the worst when they came at night.

He couldn't stay on with the Army after that. His nerves just wouldn't stand it. Everywhere around him after that night, every tree, every bush blowing in the wind unleashed a terror inside of him. It was the same terror that he experienced in his dreams now sometimes. It was well before sunset still, but wiping the last of the sweat from his brow, he got quietly out of bed anyhow, careful not to wake Bella. He knew from experience that no matter what the time, he'd not be sleeping again that night.

Gaylord made his way into the kitchen, stepping large over the loose floorboards in the entry way. He'd been meaning to fix them for about six years now, and each year the damned things only seemed to grow louder. He was supposed to have time for that sort of thing. He'd come back home after leaving Nebraska Territory, and he'd honestly thought that assuming the role of Lucas County Sheriff would be a part-time affair at best. He'd thought wrong.

If there weren't warrants that needed serving or disputes that required settling, there was court to attend to and the inmates at the jail. It seemed like there was always something that kept him from what was supposed to be his primary affair of tending his small cattle operation on the edge of town. As it was, Bella had been forced to not only provide meals to the prisoners, but also filled in as the head cattle wrangler while he was tending to his sheriff affairs and couldn't make it home.

Even if all of the regular duties hadn't been enough, about the time that he had taken office, the wars were raging along the Kansas and Missouri border. Even before there was a war that the rest of the nation was aware of men were killing each other all along the border. After the civil war broke out, things had only gotten worse.

Each day brought with it the threat of an actual invasion by secessionists out of Missouri. And even barring the weekly rumors of invasions, there had been a real threat lurking among them at night in the form of bands of horse thieves from across the border. As the war intensified, the losses only increased as anything in riding distance of the border offered fair game to Missouri marauders and horses were always in high demand.

In 1860, the Chariton chapter of the Anti Horse Thief Society was formed. By 1861, nearly every community within a day's ride of the Missouri border had formed a chapter, from Kansas to Illinois. Half posse, half militia, the Society was kept so busy that membership was limited to a one year terms of service. Horse theft, after all, was serious business, especially in poor rural areas. You steal a man's horse and you're stealing his transportation, his means of conducting businesses and farming. In country where folks didn't have much, losing a horse could mean a death sentence during the winter months for a man and his entire family.

It was serious, and the marauders who came up from Missouri knew that to be caught was to be hanged too. That meant that if you caught up to them before they made the border that you could expect men who were fighting for their very lives and knew it.

In the kitchen, Sheriff Lyman opened the door of the cook stove and threw in a few pieces of split wood from the box nearby. He left the door open and let his body absorb the heat from the coals and allowed the warm air to fill the room around him. Lighting a particularly skinny stick aflame, he removed it still burning. Then he turned and picked up the lantern from the table, stopping to pull up his suspenders and keep his pants from falling to the floor.

As the flame took and the lantern filled the dark room with flickering light, he did not so much as flinch as he saw the figure take shape before him in the doorway. It was his oldest son Jacob who stood before him. Sheriff Lyman turned back, and opening the vents on the stove to let the thing take full flame for morning, he closed the door and secured it tightly.

"Morning Jacob," he said softly to the figure behind him.

"Morning Pa," Jacob replied. "What stirs you at this hour?"

"Bad dreams son," Sheriff Lyman replied.

Both men took a seat at the table. The sheriff looked at the face of his oldest son, and awed at how at seventeen, he really had become a man. The boy was taller than himself by two inches and at 5'-11" he was considerably taller than most folks of the day.

Beyond simply being tall though, he had proven himself a responsible man at every turn. Jacob had always done well and earned good marks in school. When there were chores to be done around the farm you never even had to ask and Jacob was out doing them. He'd always been that way. For as much as Gaylord the Sheriff hadn't been around, as Jacob had aged he'd spelled his mother of most of her outside work on the farm.

Jacob, more than the others, was Gaylord's pride and joy. He might be in University somewhere too, except that Logan had hired him to work down at the creamery at fifteen. And creamery work wasn't easy by any means, even for grown men. It was hard physical labor that found you up in the morning before dawn, then home for chores only when the deliveries had been made for the day, only to find you back at the creamery again that night.

Most adult men couldn't handle the routine of the job, but Jacob never once issued a complaint about it. He only put his head down and worked. The young man gave some of his earnings to his mother for his keep too, saving every penny of the rest to eventually buy a farm to call his own. If things went well, Jacob had thought, he may even buy the creamery one day from Mr. Logan when he finally decided to quit it.

No, Gaylord couldn't help but be proud of Jacob. Any father would be proud to call him a son. But still, sitting there at the table, the Sheriff could only think of how little time he had spent with the boy. How little they really *knew* one another. He wished that he'd spent more time with him; wished that he'd talked to him more while he was growing up. But he hadn't. He'd always been gone with the Army, or gone out working to protect the county from desperados. It seemed there had always been *something* that had kept him from being there, but even in spite of his absence, Jacob had become a fine young man.

"What is it Pa?" Jacob asked as he pulled on his boots.

"What is what?" Gaylord replied, pulled back to the moment from his deep thoughts.

"Them bad dreams you have. What are they of?" Jacob replied, securing his boots firmly and turning to face his father squarely and look into his eyes.

The Sheriff began to feel uneasy. After returning from Nebraska Territory, he had never once spoken to a soul about what had happened out there. He'd never even considered it. But now, here was his son asking him about it again. He had kept it from them all a long time and he had figured that he always would. There was no sense in burdening folks with that sort of thing. Still, looking at his son and recognizing that the boy had come so far without a good father around all the time, he felt that he owed it to him. Gaylord believed that if he shared his secret with his son, it would be his way of showing Jacob how much he cared about him.

Gaylord had discovered the hard way, that with children, it isn't the things that you did wrong that bother you, but the things that you never did at all. He owed it to Jacob to tell him. Maybe it would help him understand why he kept so much inside of him. Maybe it would bring them closer together.

The Sheriff swallowed hard, and looking directly into the eyes of his son, knew the time had come to talk to him.

Chapter 3   A Cold Day In Missouri

Some forty plus miles to the southeast of the Lyman farm near Chariton, on another farm just across the Missouri line Elias Wilson rolled out of his bed and hit the floor with a thud. His mouth was dry as a bone and as his senses awakened he could smell the rank odor of dried vomit wafting up from his undershirt.

His bed was little more than an old stove crate that had been cut in half with a tack infested mattress laid over it. He called it a mattress anyways, but it too was a makeshift comprised of flour sacks that had been stitched hastily together and filled with the shake from straw and then topped with chicken feathers. It took some doing if he wasn't on a really good drunk to find a spot where some hard stick of straw did not poke him *somewhere*.

"Hiram!" he called into the empty house. "Hiram, you fetch me some water, boy!"

Sitting still, Elias listened and heard nothing from his son. There was no reply. There was no sound of anyone stirring.

"Hiram, get your behind out of bed or so help me!" With that Elias stopped yelling. He still didn't hear any movement or reply and the act of yelling made him feel as if his entire head might explode.

It was evident from the worst pounding headache he'd had in recent years that his recipe for the perfect sipping whiskey still had much to be desired. He was certain by now that the grain was correct for good mash, but there was something terribly wrong with the sifting charcoal. For not only did it taste peculiar, but it left him near incapacitated the next morning. No sense letting that batch age any longer, he'd thought to himself as he struggled to his feet. He'd have to see if he couldn't sell it to the Maddy Brothers down the road, lessen he keep it around and become tempted to sample it once more. Lord only knew that the Maddy's would drink anything you put in front of them.

Elias stumbled about the room, removing his soiled, stinking shirt. He then replaced it with another slightly less reproach-able one from the pile of dirties in the corner. Cold weather or no, it was time to see to it that Hiram did the washing again. Damn that boy, he thought. If it weren't for him telling the boy to do it, he was certain that Hiram would forget to even eat. He had always been such a queer child and he was making no better of a man at twenty years of age.

Looking back, Elias remembered his own self at twenty. He remembered working on his father's farm from sunrise until sunset. He remembered a hard, yet rewarding life of brute physical labor. Also, he remembered the brutal beatings dolled out by his father for every conceivable perceived slight. It was not uncommon to receive a blow from a buckled harness for not doing anything at all as it was for doing something wrong. In his day, things were so much harder than they were for Hiram. He'd never laid hand on the child that he didn't have it coming to him. Trouble was that he *always* had it coming though.

Stepping into the main room, Elias looked to the pile of linens in the corner that had served as Hiram's bed for some eight odd years. There was no sign of the boy. The small table and chairs that served as their supping place were lying sprawled out in disarray upon the floor. Elias imagined that he'd accidentally knocked them over the night before when he'd stumbled in, but who can remember every little thing?

Righting a chair, he reached for the water pail near the stove. The water inside of it had formed a thin layer of ice across the top that broke when he poked at it with his finger. Lifting it to his lips, he raised the entire bucket above him and drank like he'd only just emerged from the desert of Egypt. He even let the cold water and ice fragments spill around his open lips, run down upon his chest and then trickle across his belly. He inhaled deeply to catch his breath and finally set what remained of the water aside.

The cold air and the even colder water caused Elias to sit up briskly and inhale a deep breath. It was good merely to be alive after another failed experiment with the sipping whiskey. There was more than one fool soul among them who'd ventured to distill in the winter months and wound up frozen solid somewhere when they'd passed out wrong. He could still hold his whiskey though, even the bad stuff. At fifty-two years old, Elias may have felt more like seventy-two that morning, and the deep set lines upon his weary face would have caused him to look more like eighty-two, but by God, he could still hold his whiskey. At least there was that! There was, after all, something to be said about the character of a man who could do so.

"Hiram!" he screamed at the top of his rejuvenated lungs, knowing full well that the boy was holed up in the woodshed once again. "Hiram, you get in here for breakfast, damn it!"

He'd starve if you didn't remind him to eat! Elias shook his head in disgust and wondered to himself what curse was upon him to have caused such a troubled existence; the loss of his beloved Jasmine and the one thing they'd sewed together in this world being this simple headed loaf of a son that she had bore him. Elias rubbed his aching head and hollered once more for Hiram.

Head pounding, Elias looked to the heavens above him, but only stared at the cobweb covered rafters of the small cabin he had built for his bride. His wife, Jasmine, and the mother of Hiram, had died some fourteen years before. Hiram was only six on that fateful day and Elias had done everything he could for a boy that age by sending him away to live with his sister back east.

Iowa in the 1850's was no place suitable for a child without a mother, he'd figured. So, it would be best to send him off until he was old enough to help on the farm. At least that way, the child might not feel himself such a burden. What's more, Elias' sister was a devout Baptist and the strict rearing of a Baptist home would do the boy some good.

But in the end it hadn't done him any good. It hadn't done him any good at all. By the time the boy returned home at the age of eleven, he had scarcely grown an inch. He was short and puny and the city living had made him soft and dim of the wits that are required to serve as a good farm hand. He knew nothing of cattle or of hogs, of corn nor of oats, and it were even as if he'd not been in the company of any horse stock whatsoever.

So frequent was the need to correct the child when he returned home with whippings and beatings that Elias had tired himself of it mostly, and took to locking the boy in the woodshed for his punishment instead. Hiram though, strange as he was, seemed to take to it over the years and would just sort of slink off there on his own accord.

As if to further enrage Elias purposely, the slothful Hiram would be curled up in the corner of the woodshed with books and letters of all things! Books! It was almost more than a body could tolerate.

"Hiram!" he yelled once more, clutching his aching head in his hands.

Finally he could hear the creaking of the wood shed door right outside of his own. Finally his indolent sloth of a son emerged from his torpid state of repose. Then, the cabin door swung slowly open and the fruit of his loin ambled inside.

Chapter 4 Patience

Evelyn Bates was a thirty year old widow and mother of Ellis, 11. Seeing Ellis off for school, she turned her attention toward her stitching. She had always loved to stitch on hankies, sheets, even shirts. Creating beautiful designs of flowers and children playing was her only true respite from an often chaotic and stressful world. The simple act of putting needle to thread to fabric drew her attentions and enabled her to withdraw to a serenity that few other places afforded her.

More than that though, as she worked out the patterns of each color and stitch in her mind, she also seemed able to work out the troubles in her life that vexed her. Needless to say, she had done a lot of stitching since her husband Henry had died the year before.

Henry was a quiet man, seldom to anger and equally seldom to laugh. What he had lacked in excitement and emotion though, he compensated for by providing emotional stability to those around him. He was dependable, reliable, and by all accounts, a decent man. Henry had sought to rescue a mule that had slipped into a creek the winter prior. The mule made it out that day. Henry never did. He was forty-one years young.

From the day that her husband had died, a kind neighbor, Jasper Logan began tending to her farm for her. She had offered to pay him a hundred times for his services but Jasper would have none of it. Jasper was as of yet unmarried himself and at 36 years old, he seemed ready to settle down with a good woman. In fact, as of late, he'd made his intentions perfectly clear to Evelyn that he was indeed ready to settle down...with her.

Jasper was a very different man from Henry though. For one thing he was very successful and was widely considered one of Lucas County, Iowa's most eligible, and handsome, bachelors. Aside from his own three hundred acre spread, Jasper also owned Logan's Creamery in Chariton. Even with all of the work and hours involved in running your own creamery and maintaining a dairy herd, Jasper had still found time to tend to Evelyn's farm and spend a bit of time with her son, Ellis, a few days a week. She had come to wonder if the man ever even really slept at all.

Over the course of the past year her mother had tried to convince her to return to Illinois and live near the rest of the family. She had agreed only after discovering that the chores of the house and the work required to keep the farm up and running were simply too much for a single body to endure. Besides, she had burdened her neighbors, especially Jasper Logan, quite enough. With Jasper's assistance and guidance, she had begun selling off their property, lock, stock, and barrel, as it were.

Only a few days prior, they had finalized the sale of the farm itself. She and young Ellis had relocated themselves to the Harris Inn in Chariton where she announced they would be staying until Ellis completed his school year. Of course, Ellis was not the real reason behind her lingering there. She needed time to consider the offers made by her pursuer. She knew that Jasper was kind and successful and she had certainly never been courted so, but still, she remained uncertain about what sort of father he would make to Ellis. There were moments when his patience would get the better of him and she wanted to take every precaution to get to know him better before she made the leap of faith.

Faith, she had learned over the years, may move mountains and heal all wounds. But faith does nothing to prove what kind of husband and father a man will be. Her own older sister had proven that when she married Ike Brady. In school in Illinois, Ike had always been the class clown, the trickster, and the center of attention. But there was nothing funny about how the man took to the whiskey later on. There was nothing to laugh about when he beat his wife and children thus. And there was little humor on the day that he shot himself either and left them all with nothing.

No. Evelyn would not rush into anything that concerned her future or the well being of young Ellis. She was content to stitch from her third floor room at the Harris Inn for a hundred years if she must, if that is what it took to be sure of the internal character of Jasper Logan.

Besides, child in tow or not, Mrs. Evelyn Bates, at a mere thirty years of age, had come into her own. She was widely considered the prettiest woman in all of Lucas County. And beyond that, unlike most women, she knew it. Her long black wavy hair shone in the sun like a glistening star and drew the attention of every man around. Not to mention her sparkling, bright blue eyes and warm smile.

Evelyn could melt the heart of anyone she met with a simple smile. She had spent a lifetime honing the arts of her subtle charms. So while the handsome and successful likes of Jasper

Logan might be enough to sweep most any girl off of her feet without a second thought, Evelyn was content to wait and be oh, so certain that he was indeed, the *one* for her. Besides, what girl did not enjoy making a man pursue her with ardent fervor?

Looking out the laced curtains into the shining rays of the early morning sun, Evelyn smiled warmly in admiration of her mastery of the virtue of patience. Time, she thought, would reveal all and answer all her questions. She had never been so certain of herself in her life. She knew without doubt that the hand of the Lord and the watchful eye of her departed husband must be guiding her through her thoughts and decisions.

Looking away, she reached for her yellow threaded needle and set about to stitch a rising morning sun behind the scene on the fabric in her lap. Patience, she thought to herself, and then she sewed another tiny stitch into her elaborate design.

Chapter 5   Confessions

Sheriff Gaylord Lyman had asked his son to wait while he had brewed them a pot of coffee. As the coffee had percolated, Jacob went to the privy outside and then joined his father back at the kitchen table. By that time however, Solomon had risen as well. Solomon was Gaylord's middle son. At fifteen he was the spitting image of his father at the same age; tall and slender with an ornery smile and difficult disposition.

For as much as Jacob, the eldest, had worked to please those around him in life and make everyone, including himself, proud of his deeds and actions. Solomon, or Sol as his family referred to him, did as he saw fit at every turn. If Sol determined it to be too nice of a day to attend school and make his marks, he'd simply go fishing that day instead. When Sol didn't see the use in learning his Latin in school, he'd simply not go that day.

When his father took the belt to him for ditching, Sol would seem relatively unmoved. It was as if there was no reproach, no punishment that could move the boy to action or against his own strong will. For all of his efforts with Sol, Gaylord felt as if he had failed at every turn. In the end, however, Sol was turning into a remarkable young man in his own right despite it all. The Sheriff could take a wild stallion, or face off with a band of gun wielding desperados, but the daily management of Sol had perplexed him beyond his own limited abilities as a father.

"Good," Gaylord smiled uncomfortably at his two oldest sons. After pouring them each a cup of hot coffee, he reached across the small table and touched each of their hands as he looked in their eyes.

"What is it Pa?" Sol asked, still rubbing the sleep from his eyes.

"Shhhh. Quiet Sol. Pa is about to tell us something," Jacob interjected, staring in quiet awe at the expression on his Father's face.

Jacob knew that this moment was a rare one in their lives. He could see that this was going to be important. He recognized it by his Pa's face, by the expression as it changed from its usual apparent concrete certainty, into something more vulnerable than Jacob had ever seen him wear before.

"You boys remember the dirt house in Nebraska Territory?" he began. Both boys nodded their heads in affirmation. He was certain that Solomon couldn't really remember living there as he was only three, but he'd heard enough stories about it that it had become like his own memory.

"Well," began the Sheriff, "during that time out there your Ma and I were homesteading a little piece of ground right across the Nebraska border. Things weren't going so good for us so I figured that I'd do a bit with the Army because they were always looking for folks to do all sorts of things.

I never went regular Army really. I was more of a conscript soldier. Sure enough, I had to deal with all the regular Army regulations and such and there's plenty to be said about all of that, but this story isn't about those things.

It was early in the spring of 58', too early to be out in the territory really because out there the spring could whip up a storm to rival anything that came in the winter time. But still, it had been a hard winter and we needed the extra pay that the duty would provide so I volunteered to go on a small mapping expedition into the heart of the Territory.

By then, there were already small settlements throughout the Territory; tiny groups of cabins along rivers and traders who had been there since the beginning of time. We weren't part of a regular Army movement. Fell, we weren't even a scouting detail. In fact, there were only the five of us. There were a couple of cartographers and a surveyor, and a single Army officer who could translate if it were needed named Lieutenant Richards, and me, who went along as a cook and stock tender mostly. In fact, by that time, they had changed regulations and I wasn't even required to wear a uniform any more because I wasn't an Army regular.

It was just the year prior that some 35 hearty souls had ventured out from Iowa into the Territory and settled on a spot they called La Grande Island. Their cabins were like an oasis in the desert along the Platte River Road, too. We stayed among them for a few days before we lit out and enjoyed some of the finest food I had ever eaten. They was Germans, and say what you will about them Germans, they cook some mean vittles.

Anyhow, our charge was to set a course to the North and East from there across land. There was at that time, still a lot of ground that hadn't been laid to paper and it seemed like the

Army wasn't satisfied until they knew every nook and cranny of a place.

We had ridden for four days straight in that direction against the warnings of the La Grande Islanders, who had warned us that there was heavy fighting going between the Lakota Sioux and the Pawnee to the north of them.

We didn't pay it no mind though because we were a small party and anyone could see that we weren't out looking for a fight. Besides, there were hundreds of Indians living all along the Missouri River then that we had encountered frequently and they were all real easy to get along with. A lot of folks cursed them, but they were always decent to us in our dealings so I wasn't in the least bit afraid.

Finally, after those last four days of riding, we stopped and made camp where their maps left off and the unknown began. Out there you can see for fifty miles boys. I mean, you can pick a spot on the horizon and ride all day for it and be just as close as you was that morning when the sun goes down. It's sandy like the desert and the only thing growing is scrub brush for miles around.

In the day it gets hot, real hot, and it dries your mouth something fierce. Then at night the winds come out of no-where and the temperature drops fifty or sixty degrees. That's why we picked us a spot in a bottom to camp. Usually you like to pick a spot atop a knoll or something where you can see around you, but we had to hunker down out of the winds to keep warm, you see.

Anyhow, we settled in and pitched our tents and I started rounding up dinner after I unloaded the mules and got the horses cared for. I remember thinking that even though the weather was terrible and the land was barren that it was probably one of the most beautiful places I had ever seen. I remember thinking that a body could almost reach out and touch the evening sky. I've never seen a bigger sky anywhere in all of my life, boys. And when the sun started to set into the horizon, it was as if you were viewing a real life scene from one of the gospels. I aim to tell you it was incredible."

Sheriff Lyman paused to take a long, thoughtful sip from his coffee. He had been talking for a spell already in his slow, deep methodic voice. He had always had a way of speaking that drew in his listener because he thought before he spoke and he didn't waste his words often as many folks seemed to do those days. When Sheriff Lyman talked, people leaned in to listen.

His sons that morning were no exception. Each of them dangled on his every syllable as if their very lives hung at the end of each sentence. Sol was about to piss himself from the beginning, but he managed to ignore the call of his body as he feared missing even a word or losing the rare moment altogether when his father actually took the time to speak to them in earnest.

Gaylord Lyman lowered the cup and swallowed the warm coffee. Most of the heat had steamed out of it while he had talked. It reminded him of the trail coffee that he had made that night so long ago in the Nebraska Territory. It too, had been piss warm and thick as tar. He had always made his coffee blacker than most folks could handle it. Closing his eyes he could almost taste the salted pork they'd had for dinner that night out there on the prairie too.

Opening his eyes again, he continued without looking up. He wasn't sure he could even form the words of the rest of the story and look his sons in the eyes. There was so much that he was ashamed of about it even then. There was so much that he had tried for so many years not to think of, let alone speak of.

Gaylord swallowed the rest of his coffee in a gulp, exhaled deeply, and continued to tell the tale. It was time they knew.

Chapter 6   Hiram's Vengeance

Hiram Wilson heard his father yelling at him and sat up in his bed. It wasn't a bed really, but rather, just a large pile of blankets and furs that he had bundled in a corner of the wood shed. His father had taken to locking him in there years before. There were times when he would lock him inside then go on a drunk somewhere and forget about him altogether. It didn't take many times of that before Hiram began stocking a hidden hoard of the necessities of life alongside a few secret items he kept to pass the time.

Among the secret stuff were a book that he had found that had belonged to his departed Mother and letters that he had received from Clara. Those, he treasured more than anything in this world and he kept them tucked away in a box hidden in the wall of the structure where his father would never find them.

Hiram was blessed by his time with his aunt in Illinois only to the extent that he had learned how to read, and it was there that he had met Clara. For as much as the abuse from his

37

father was routine and often came without rhyme or reason, life at his Aunt Ethel's home was far worse. Ethel was a strict Baptist and beatings were dolled out there with the fervor of a missionary torturing his subjects into submission.

She would beat him for not eating his beans one night, then beat him the next for eating his beans too quickly. The worst of it however, had been that every beating, every punishment meted out, brought with it a sermon and more lines from the scripture that he was forced to try and memorize before morning.

Of course, there was seldom a night when he could find the time or the concentration required to memorize any God damned scripture, so come morning he'd receive another beating for not having memorized the thing. It was like that every day at his Aunt Ethel's house. Every day a new set of rules to live by, and every day a new set of whippings with leather straps or wooden canes or whatever was handy. But always, the sermons during the whippings were the worst part. He'd as soon have been beaten clear to death than have to listen to that old hag carry on about her God ever again.

Hiram had risen from his blanket pile, carefully folding the letter from Clara he'd been reading the night before. Her letters always had a way of comforting him when he needed it most. Truly, she was the only thing soft, the only thing tender and nurturing that existed in his life. Her words were the wings that could carry him away from everything else. In the evenings when things were particularly bad, he could hold her letters and read them again and again. He could imagine how her soft, tiny hand had folded that very piece of parchment not so long before. And during the days, the words that she had placed upon that parchment would echo in his mind. It was then that he could hear the sweetness of her voice as if she were right there behind him whispering them into his ear.

Hiram neatly folded the letter and placed it back into the carefully opened envelope it had arrived in. As he received each new letter, he would first sharpen his pocket knife to ensure a clean cut, then slice gently along the seam at one end. This was not only to perfectly preserve each treasure that had once touched her hand, but also because he had discovered that by leaving the envelopes in tact, he could open one end and smell inside, giving him a faint hint of the perfumed powder that had adorned her body on the day that she had sent the letter. Hiram could feel his heart beating in his chest whenever he stuck his nose inside an envelope. If he was careful with them, the smell could last for weeks. Closing his eyes before he put the letter away, he exhaled and envisioned Clara smiling as she had penned the letter and thought of him.

Gently, Hiram set the letter inside the cigar tin with the others and placed it in the tiny nook inside the wood shed wall. The wood shed had once actually been a small dwelling that the first squatter on their parcel had called his home. It was a mere 8 feet long by just as many wide, but the inside of it had been lined with rough hewn native timbers, and the joints between them caulked with lime.

Working with only his knife years before, Hiram had cut loose a single plank that ran the length of the interior. He had been careful too, to cut away the caulked joint so that it remained intact and could be removed and replaced without being noticeably different from the others. At times, pieces of caulking would break away from the wood, and Hiram would carefully glue them back into place along the top of the board.

It was such attention to detail that had allowed him to keep hidden his treasures and food stores that were required to make his prison more like a home to him. He had even constructed a tiny stove of sorts out of a small can. He found that by dousing fabric shreds in lantern oil, and packing them very tightly into the can, that it would produce a small heat source that would burn for hours just hot enough to take the freezing bite off of the air that filled his tomb.

Hiram replaced the coarse wood plank in the wall concealing his stash of goods and treasures. He took note of the fact that the rough hewn board was beginning to appear slightly smoother than the rest from the wear and oil from his own hands. He would have to scuff it up, he had thought, and probably rub lard over the entire wall to conceal the differences.

He stood for a moment thinking of how he would go about it all, then turned away to go inside the house where his father sat calling his name. Hiram carried with him a small bundle of split wood to stoke the stove with inside. He also grabbed a handful of smaller sticks to use as tinder for he doubted that even embers would have remained since the evening before. He knew that his father would not have roused to tend the fire.

Hiram opened the door of the shed and the cold, early morning air blew in and filled his room. Stepping outside, he could see a bit of the glow of the morning sun shining through the wintry haze, but nothing more. He stepped outside on to the hard packed snow that served as his short trail between the tiny structure they called a home, and his even tinier shed that he had come to call a refuge.

It had been intended to serve as his prison, his place of punishment. Instead he had transformed it into a place of solitude, a place of refuge from the abuse of his father and the harshness of the world outside. Once more, Hiram glanced back inside at the board that held all of his worldly treasures and secured the door closed behind hem.

It was but fifteen short steps to the cabin, but even such a short distance in the bitter wind was enough for the cold to breech his clothes. He shivered as he approached the cabin and paused only momentarily to look across their snow covered yard and to the scattered elm trees that lined the fence to the fields beyond.

The elm trees stood, devoid of foliage and seemingly equally devoid of life itself. They were to him as the skeletons of giant stags, with bony antlers projecting into the sky and serving as foreboding warnings to any who neared, as if they were frightening harbingers in the winter sky that served to keep anything good, anything descent, from entering on to their property and into their lives.

Hiram turned away from the trees and opened the door to the cabin where he paused momentarily, allowing his eyes to adjust to the darkness inside. For even what little light the glow of the morning sun had shed upon him, it was enough to blind him to the darkness that awaited him inside the cabin. But the lack of light inside, he knew all too well, was not the only darkness that awaited him there and gave him pause. And, as if on cue from the orations of a vaudeville narrator, the *other* darkness spoke.

"What the hell has been keeping you boy?!" Elias screamed at him, but the phlegm in his dry throat caused his voice to crackle before he could scream the entire sentence at the level he had meant to convey it. "Haven't you heard me calling for you?"

"No, sir," Hiram replied, stepping inside the cabin. "I come soon as I heard you, Pa."

"Close the God damned door you stupid oaf!" Elias yelled, having cleared his throat. "Is it your aim to freeze me to death?"

"No, sir," Hiram replied once more. Closing the door behind him and stepping toward the stove.

"What the hell are you doing out there anyhow? Are you so simple in the head that you won't even freeze to death?" His father queried. "Can it be that by simply being so ignorant of the ways a man meets his demise, that a fool might be slow enough in the head as to thwart those ways, and cheat even death in the same way that he cheats me out of an honest day's work?"

"I don't know, sir," Hiram replied quietly. Turning away from the tirade, he knelt and creaked open the heavy cast iron door of the stove. Reaching inside the thing with a poker he discovered that things were not as bad as they had first seemed as he shook the ash and discovered a few dull glowing embers buried among them.

Reaching above him, Hiram adjusted open the vent and as the air wafted through the chamber the embers began to glow to life once more. Carefully he arranged his tinder atop them so that they would catch the heat and flame from the glowing miracles, but not deprive them of the flow of air that breathed the life into them.

"You answer me boy!" Elias yelled, throwing the empty water pail at him. The pail struck Hiram in the back of the head.

Hiram was uninjured by the thing as it bore little weight but he turned as a wildcat toward his father, ready to flee or defend his life from the next blow. As the flames took in open stove behind him they cast a light into the room and the murky shadow of the figure at the table began to take shape and grow details. He could see that his father was of little threat that morning, as the very act of throwing the pail caused him to lose his breath and grasp at his aching head.

"I was in the shed last night by your hand, Pa," he replied. "You come home late last night in fine form. You threw about the kitchen chairs, and toppled the table here, and you come to my corner and took your boots to me. I was in the shed because you had me remove me to the shed when you come home. Don't you remember, Pa?"

It was but a tiny jab, but at times, tiny victories were the best ones, or at least the only ones that were within Hiram's grasp. His father, for all of his drunkenness, for day after day of beginning each morning with a biscuit and a jug of whiskey, deplored the thought that he might be a drunkard of any sort. Elias could not imagine himself amongst the men who drunk themselves to sleep each night under the boardwalks of the towns in front of the saloons, even as he himself had awakened there on more than one occasion. Still, he reckoned to cast himself of a different, better lot, than them wretched souls.

But Hiram knew better. He knew what he really was and he took increasing advantage (and delight) of any opportunity to thrust imperceptibly tiny, phonic spears into his father's facade. He knew it, and knew it all too well that any mention of drunkenness or even the slightest indication that he may have misplaced several hours of his actions as a result of it, would settle poorly upon his father's aching head.

"Don't I remember?!?!" his father scoffed defensively. "Why, you lousy ingrate! I had ought to bust that mouth of yours with a chunk of oak from the shed there yonder from whence you have crawled on this day!"

"I'm sorry, Sir," Hiram replied coyly, adding larger pieces to the flames and balancing an even larger chunk upon the top of his tiny pyre. "I didn't mean it so."

"You are a sorry lot indeed," his father rebuked. I remember returning home sure enough to find the place in a shameful state of disrepair. I remember all too well kicking the sloth from his place of slumber too! It served you well to sleep the night with the rats too, boy!"

"Yes, sir," Hiram replied quietly. "I reckon it did, at that."

His father sunk his head into his hands as if beaten down by the one sided arguing. It was more than his head could take on that day. Hiram only smiled slightly at the tiny victory that he had scored for himself as he began to mix the morning biscuits. Once they were settled and baking, he would go out to fetch the eggs and pay visit to the privy house.

It was an all too familiar routine that his life had become of surprise midnight beatings followed by scornful, hateful morning tongue lashings. As the day progressed and the older man's hangover gave way to drunkenness, more beatings would ensue until Hiram was once again in his wood shed and his father had left the place in drunken disgust, off to malinger with others of his own pathetic ilk.

"Soon, my sweet Clara," he said. "We'll be together soon my love," Hiram whispered aloud to himself. He dreamed that his words would flow upon the cold westerly winds and set upon her ear later that very morning back in Illinois.

Looking back down to the biscuit batter, he glanced behind him to his father who appeared to be asleep once more, head upon his arms at the rough hewn kitchen table. Hiram turned his back to the sleeping drunkard and for good measure, spat into two of the biscuits before placing them quietly upon the stove so as not to rouse the old man. With the biscuits finished, Hiram left to tend to the chickens.

Chapter 7   Successful Foundation

Shortly after the hour that men like Elias Wilson had finally stumbled in and found their beds, Jasper Logan was getting out of his. He had three secrets to his success that he had never shared with anyone. All of them had to do with the hours he was able to keep. Chariton, Iowa in 1870 was a place that was ripe for the plucking. By Jasper's account, men who thought that success required luck would always find themselves to be unlucky in the end.

Success, in that time and place required no such an animal as luck. It required no capital, no fortune to be born into. For the first, and perhaps the last, a brief window of place and time emerged where a man need only be industrious to become successful. The wealth and holdings of any man fortunate enough to have been born right then and right there, would be equivalent to his own ambitions and determination. Thus were the beliefs of Jasper Logan, and those beliefs had served him well in his 36 short years on this earth.

Already he had amassed more land than a man could walk the circumference and interior of in a single day, and far more than a body could work independently. In addition, he had evolved from a farmer into a respected dairy farmer and breeder of the most admired milk producers in the southern tiers of Iowa counties. As if that were not enough, Jasper had reckoned the difference between the farmer's take on a gallon of milk or quart of butter to be too insignificant when inspected beside the creamery's cut of the same, so he simply edged out the middle man and opened the doors of his own creamery in Chariton.

With the Logan name attached to it, and his reputation as a breeder of such fine animals, the Logan Creamery had little apparent difficulty in rapidly becoming *the* place for city dwellers in the county to purchase their milk, cream and butter from. In 1868, he had even built on to the establishment and employed a butcher as well. Aside from the Logan name, the entire enterprise was aided by the fact that every worker received a share of the operation. Every employee could depend upon a fat check at the end of the month when business was good, and at Logan's business was always good.

Jasper, through his own hard work, and by operating in a way to make his workers stock holders, had broken barriers of even his own expectations. In fact, as his co-owners had begun to complain of the rates at the local savings and loan, Jasper was even planning to open their own bank to compete. That is how the world worked in Jasper's mind; you worked hard and you reaped the benefits of your efforts. If something still didn't suit you, you simply worked a little harder and changed the thing.

Indeed, it was a world ripe for the plucking! Even all of that were not the real secrets of his success though. The real secrets lie in his ability to suck the very marrow out of every single day, to get the good out of every hour. In a world where industry equaled success, the most of it would always be reserved for he who worked the hardest AND the longest.

Jasper Logan, as it turned out had three simple secrets behind his accomplishments, and they were as closely guarded as any king's treasure. They were simple really, almost comical. Still, they were the secrets that had made him what he had become, and it was upon those very secrets that he had laid the foundations of a local American Empire.

Logan rose from his bed that morning long before any rooster even dared to stir. As he did each morning, he stepped outside on his porch in his long johns only and walking to the edge, stood in the briskness of the cold air, letting it fill his lings while he urinated into the snow. Therein lay the first secret. Logan had a very small, very weak bladder. This seeming curse of a bladder had caused him to wet himself each night until the age of fourteen when he finally learned to awaken and rise to see to its discharge.

As it came to pass in his teen years and later as an adult however, that same small bladder served as his own internal clock. It gave him the natural ability to tell, despite the lack of sunlight cast upon the world, what time of the morning it was. He had discovered that by simply following a routine whereby he urinated and then consumed a glass of warm buttermilk right before bed, he would be certain to rise around three in the morning.

The next secret was really a number of things all rolled into one secret. For, while he had early on learned to rise before most, it took time to draft the perfect recipe for staying awake. The first part of that secret was in stretching outdoors in his underwear each morning and taking in the fresh air regardless of the season. The next 'ingredient' was his coffee. In addition to making some of the thickest, blackest tar that a body could imagine brewing and still being able to call it a 'drink', Logan would purposely deposit fresh grounds into every single cup that he drank. These, he chewed after drinking the cup. He sucked them and savored them. He worked them into a tiny ball and placed them along his cheek as if they were a chaw of tobacco. And when they had become devoid of any juices, when every last drop of flavor had been drained from them, he swallowed them.

As a young man, he had told a friend about this curious custom of his and the friend had been so awestruck and disgusted by it, that Logan had never divulged it to anyone again. What's more, he added it to the entire list of habits and quirks that he maintained and sealed them all tightly into a locked iron box inside of his mind, reserved as the secrets that set himself apart from the rest, and keys to making him the most envied man in the county.

Jasper's final and perhaps most closely guarded secret was that in his office at the creamery, there was a hidden room behind it. There, beyond the eyes of anyone, and in the most secretive environment possible, where no one would ever discover him, Jasper Logan slipped quietly away from his desk, twice each day, and for twenty minutes a turn, he took a nap upon a stuffed burlap mattress.

It was shameful thing really, the man who was widely known as the most industrious body in all of Lucas County; a man who many suspected of never sleeping at all. That such a man would skulk away in secret and take a nap! For as much as the day favored hard work and industry above all else, napping was considered by most folks to be the devil's work. A nap was clearly the antithesis of labor, as if Satan himself had laid low the otherwise righteous and purposeful soul with the seduction of mere pure idle laziness. For Jasper Logan though, it was this unique blend of coffee grounds, fresh air, a weak bladder, and naps that allowed him to work some twenty hours out of each and every day, and amass a growing fortune whilst other men slept each night.

Whatever his secrets, everyone agreed that Japer Logan had laid the foundations of a life well lived and full of reward. To the citizens of Chariton, he was a body to be envied and an example of industry for the little children and loafing husbands. To Jasper it was not enough. It would never be enough. All of the money and land and business ventures could not fill the void in his life. One thing had been missing through it all, and that one thing was Evelyn Bates.

As it turned out, Napping was not Jasper's only sin. Because since the day that he had first set eyes upon Evelyn, he had secretly coveted another man's wife. He had never made mention of it to anyone, but every time that he saw her smile it set a flame inside of belly and an aching inside his heart that would last him for days upon end. A simple "hello" from Evelyn on the street in Chariton and that amazing smile of hers would find him laying awake at night and going without even his customary few hours of sleep for several days on end.

What was the sense of it all, he had wondered. What good is building a grand house if not for the perfect woman to share it with as a home? What sense is there in amassing a fortune without the perfect mate for your own soul to assist you in spending it? For in the construction of his own home, he could plainly see that the grandest, most extravagant parlor window adorned with the most luxurious stained glass was nothing without the laced curtains that a woman's hand would create. Certainly, a man of means could simply go and buy the curtains, but it was not the same as the ones that had been sewn and placed just so by a woman, by *the* woman of the house. His windows remained open and his heart remained empty, and he had years ago decided that only Evelyn could fill the voids.

He knew it to be so even when nothing in this world made it seem even of the remotest of possibilities. He believed it in his heart, even as the couple bore a son. When her husband had died unexpectedly, while he was genuinely sad for her and her loss, Jasper Logan had also viewed the event as a sort of divine intervention. It was as if the foundations he had laid for the perfect life, as if all of his efforts and labors and good deeds, were being rewarded by some celestial being who shared in his belief that hard work and perseverance will trump all else in the world. Live right, work hard, and all else, even matters of the heart and of the soul, will fall into place like well cut stones upon the foundations of a mighty structure.

Finally, Evelyn Bates would be his.

Chapter 8   Telling The Tale

Sheriff Gaylord Lyman looked up from his coffee and into the eyes of Sol first, then Jacob. The boys sat staring back at him, eyes wide with anticipation. He looked back down at the ripples of his coffee as it settled back into his cup on the table.

"It was shortly after we had finished our dinners that night. In fact, I had just finished stowing our things when Lieutenant Richards went to his saddle pack. The other three were sitting around the fire at the time talking about their maps and the route they would take in the morning. One of the fellas was sorting and unraveling chains that would be used to measure distances while they talked.

I had gone over by them to listen. They was a serious bunch really, very professional and even though maps and such aren't very exciting to me, the earnestness of the men made me more inquisitive than I usually would have been. I mean, they really believed in the importance of what they were about to do. Standing there under the fading light of the Nebraska sky and listening to them fellas sort of made me feel like what we were doing out there was going to really change the world.

51

It was as if we were the next Lewis and Clark or the next Christopher Columbus. I had never thought about it before then, but what lay over the next bend could be something that no white man had ever set eyes upon. It was an exciting and wondrous journey that we had embarked upon and I felt like I was making history just by being along for the ride and making dinner that night.

So, that was how I was feeling when the Lieutenant come back from his saddle bags with the jugs. Mind you, I had never been a drinking man. I might have taken a nip once or twice before that night in my whole life. But there was something so special about the night, that it seemed like a celebration of sorts was in order. And I wasn't the only one who must've felt that way either, because soon we were all taking long pulls from those jugs and laughing and sharing stories.

It was odd for a group like that to start getting friendly the way we done that night too. Back then, in the Army, you could ride with a man for weeks and never get to know him really. And an officer or professional fellas like surveyors and cartographers; well, you could ride with that sort for months and never even know their first names.

It was only in light of the evening though and the spirit of the thing, that we all let loose. We all drank a lot more and a lot faster than anyone should, but not one of us stopped to think about what we were doing. I remember that we were all laughing though and having quite a time of it.

I would reckon, looking back, that I was the first one to fall down and not get up again. I remember the others were still talking and laughing and whooping and hollering while I was laying there staring up at the stars. They were so big and bright and I remember they were spinning faster and faster on account of how drunk I was.

The next thing I remember was opening my eyes to the burning brightness of a late morning Nebraska sun. I opened them first thing and was blinded for quite a spell because of it. So I just sort of lay there for a bit, feeling the dull aching in my head and the dryness of my mouth. It was as if I had spent the entire night sucking on alum, I was so dry.

While I lay there with my eyes closed I began to notice some other things. I began to notice the buzzing of flies all about me. I could smell a thick stench in the air. It wasn't a rotten smell, but it as if someone had butchered a cow nearby. It was the thought of something that caused me to sit up abruptly as I recognized what the smell was that filled my nostrils."

Just then Sheriff Gaylord Lyman's wife, Bella walked into the room. As if a tap had been turned in a barrel keg, the Sheriff switched expressions and all of the sadness was gone from his face. He sniffled once, then turned and smiled brightly and cheerfully at Bella as she walked in. Jacob and Sol sat, jaws agape, staring at their father.

"What's going on out here?" Bella inquired.

"We was just sharing stories and some coffee, Mother," Gaylord replied to his wife as he rose from his chair and kissed her upon the cheek. "I believe that Jacob was just fixing to head on to the creamery."

"Oh lands yes, Jacob," she said, looking to the sunlight that had only just begun to fill the window pane in the kitchen. "You had best be getting along I should think."

Jacob rose from his chair and drew a deep breath. As he exhaled, he let loose the nervous tension that had filled the air of the kitchen that morning as his father had begin to share the story with them. He wiped it from his face just as his father had done before him and kissed his mother on the cheek as well.

"Yes, I should, Mama," he said. "I love you."

"I love you too son," she replied.

Jacob turned, gave his father a respectful glance and then turned to the door to head to Logan's Creamery.

Sol only sat there for a moment, mouth agape and wondered where such a story could be going. What was it that had filled his father's nostrils? What the hell had happened out there on that prairie to unnerve him so? His father was Sheriff Gaylord Lyman after all. The man was a stoic rock with nerves of steel. He was the man who other men in the community turned to when they needed someone to lean on. He was the one who counseled other men, who stood unshaken in the face of any danger, any foe.

Before that morning, Sol would have bet a king's fortune that his father had never been shaken by anything. But then he was only overwhelmed with the desire to know what exactly had happened out there. It consumed his thoughts and try as he might, he could not remove the question from the front of his mind.

The Sheriff emptied his coffee pot and started a new brew on the stove of a lighter hue for Bella and Sol to drink with their breakfast. It was time for him to be heading into town. The chores would be left for Sol. Gaylord reminded him to saddle his horse and go check on the cow he had seen staggering the day before. It wasn't a stagger per say as of yet, but there was definitely something wrong with the way the she had been walking.

Kissing Bella once more, Gaylord turned and headed out the door. They lived just on the east edge of Chariton and more often than not, Sheriff Lyman chose to walk to his office in the county courthouse. The county kept for him a horse in the livery just south of the town square anyhow, and the walk was hardly worth the saddling of a horse. Especially if he had no immediate plans to go any further for the day.

Walking through the hard packed snow, the aging Sheriff gave notice to the fact that the old cow was not the only thing walking funnier those days. At 42 years old, Gaylord was beginning to feel the effects of younger days spent breaking ponies, and legs. Each winter the pain in his aching bones and joints 'talked' to him more and more. It was beginning to show in his slow waddling amble of a walk.

Following the same trail in the road that had been plowed by Jacob's footsteps just before him, Sheriff Lyman headed into town. Already, he was beginning to regret having begun the telling of the tale. Not because he didn't want his sons to know. He wanted to try and bridge the gap that his busy life had put between them and he knew that it would help to begin to do that. Still, he had no desire to keep having to remember those things, or to think of them at all. It was all he could do to keep from breaking down when he sat and thought of them. Not that he could ever forget what had happened out there in Nebraska Territory. No, he was constantly reminded of it in his dreams. But not forgetting and intentionally remembering were two completely different things.

Ahead of him in the road, Gaylord could see through the windy winter haze of blowing snow as the figure that he was certain to be Jacob, turned south and headed for Logan's Creamery. No sooner did he see the boy, than a stiff gust churned up the dried powder before him and blew it into his face. The Sheriff stopped momentarily to let the wind pass, and turned away from it to shield his face from the stinging cold.

There, standing at the edge of a timber that was known locally as Baker's Grove, he looked down and across the frozen tundra of the old city lake. It wasn't much of a lake really, more of a pond of about four acres. He could see the square scars on the surface of it where men had been harvesting ice blocks all throughout the winter. He marveled at how the thing could maintain its' mass with so many loads of ice harvested from its waters. It was as if the thing would simply boil up from below to fill its' own reservoir again each night. He'd have thought that with so many thousands of blocks taken from the surface, and so many of hundreds of wagon loads required to fill the ice house across town that there could not possibly be anything left. But still, there it was, shining fresh ice gleaning in the early morning sun.

There were so many mysteries in this world like that one. The Sheriff felt that he was only beginning to touch upon the tip of knowing so many things. Maybe it was the ice in the pond or the beginning of the telling of the tale that he should never have lived to tell, but either way, he felt a renewed sense of gratitude for simply being alive.

He was grateful for the day, cold as it was and he smiled warmly as he walked along, eager to embrace it. He had walked and ridden a hundred dusty trails in his life, but finally he felt that he was beginning to grasp the meaning of it all. He had worked hard enough for long enough and achieved everything he had set out to in this world, save one thing. He had not been the father to his sons, or the husband to Bella that he had always desired to be.

He had the respect of the entire county, a beautiful farm to call his own, and an elected position of leadership in the community. Still, he remained unfulfilled in a way that he was only beginning to understand. Life was full of mysteries sure enough, but the greatest part about those mysteries, the most exciting thing about the beauty all around him everyday, was in the sharing them with the ones that you loved.

A block beyond Logan's Creamery, Sheriff Lyman turned south and headed toward the courthouse. The jail had been empty for weeks and the town quiet for the most part. That left him free to begin his morning just the way he enjoyed them most; with a trip to the courthouse and a hot cup of coffee with the men who assembled there with the rising suns.

He was going to miss his mornings at the courthouse. Still, it was time. He had more important work to do; things that he put aside long enough. It was that morning, walking through the sleepy town of Chariton and looking into the lantern lit windows that he past that he knew that it was due time. In home after home, children were readying to go to school and families could be seen sitting together sharing stories and breakfast alike. It was then that he knew for certain that this would be his last year as Sheriff.

In the fall, he had decided matter of fact and most suddenly, that as his term expired that autumn, so too would his time as the Sheriff of Lucas County, Iowa. By that time next year, he would be Gaylord Lyman, private citizen, farmer, husband, and father, and not necessarily in that order. As he crossed the frozen mud of the street and on to the courthouse lawn, he could smell the coffee and oak burning in the stoves inside. Yes, winter cold or not, it was going to be a very fine day.

Chapter 9 Letters

Hiram Wilson had been out in the barn forking hay and grinding corn that day for feed when he heard the familiar ringing of the bells. It was the sleigh bells of Mr. Glenn, the postmaster coming down the lane. Hiram dropped the cobs he was about to strip of kernels and ran outside to greet him. By then, the winds had subsided and leaving the barn, Hiram was greeted by a bright, blinding winter sun reflecting off of the snow.

Running out the lane so his father would not hear the bells of the sleigh, Hiram greeted Mr. Glenn almost at the road. It was amazing how far the sounds of such small bells could travel through the countryside in the winter time. There had been days when Hiram had run out to greet them, only to discover that they were in fact ringing from as much as two miles away. This, he only knew for certain because the valley below their homestead offered a full view of the winding Bell Farm road as it rose up through the timber almost a full two miles from the Wilson spread.

"Good day to you, Mr. Wilson!" Mr. Glenn greeted him cheerfully. Mr. Glenn was always cheerful and he always had greeted Hiram as "Mr. Wilson", even when he was only a small boy.

"Good day to you, Mr. Glenn!" Hiram replied enthusiastically. "Have you anything for me today, sir?"

"You know Mr. Wilson," he replied with a bright smile, "I believe that I do have something for you. Tis a letter and it would appear to be in the hand of a young woman!" With that he produced a letter from his inside coat pocket.

Mr. Glenn always put the next farm's mail inside of his coat pocket while he read. He was most diligent in doing so each and every time too, as he believed that it added to the mystique of the postal service. To him, it was as if he were carrying secret messages or highly urgent dispatches sent from high ranking generals in each piece of mail. It was a prideful thing sure enough, but it was not a sinful pride in that his pride was in the uniform, in the position, in the importance of his work and the service that was provided.

Hiram quickly took the letter from him and inspected it. He didn't even try to conceal the smile upon his face as he tucked the thing into his own inside coat pocket. It was very much as if Mr. Glenn's secret dispatch was just that, and it had only passed off from one spy to another.

"How goes your father today, Mr. Wilson?" Mr. Glenn inquired.

"He is quite well and inside the house, sir," Hiram replied.

"Well, I suppose that I should go inside and take a coffee with him then," Mr. Glenn began to climb off of his sleigh. "That way he shan't be suspicious at having heard my bells and received no mail for himself." With that he looked Hiram directly in the eye and patted him on the shoulder, flashing a bright smile and a wink as he passed.

Mr. Glenn had a smile as bright as the full moon and every time he smiled his cheeks blushed beat red until they shone through his thick white beard and handled moustache.
He was a fine man and there were entire weeks during the winter months that he would be the only other body that Hiram would get to speak to besides his father. Enough, so that Hiram was always joyful to see the cheerful man.

"He would like that, Mr. Glenn. Shall I let him know you are coming?" Hiram asked after him.

"No thank you Mr. Wilson," Mr. Glenn replied, walking stiff legged toward the cabin from having ridden too many miles in the cold. "I reckon I shall keep him occupied with my stories whilst you steal away and learn of the contents of that letter I should think!"

Hiram did not reply as Mr. Glenn had already made it to the door of the cabin and had swung it open. He would never have entered unannounced that way had it been a home with a woman of the house, but as it were he simply opened the door and disappeared inside. As Hiram quietly opened the door of the wood shed, he could already hear the two men inside of the cabin talking loudly and exchanging stories and probably a drink of Elias' latest concoction.

Closing the door of the old shed behind him, Hiram waited for his eyes to adjust to the darkness once more before striking a match to light the old oil lantern that he kept hung above him. As the lantern took and the room filled with flickering light a mouse disappeared hurriedly behind the boards that separated the dried wood pile from the rest of the small room.

Removing his pocket knife, Hiram carefully cut open the end of the letter. As he opened it, he stuck his nose inside and smelled inside. The smell of spring Lilac blooms filled his nose and he inhaled it like a dying man drawing his last deep breath before passing through to the great unknown. Clara was heavenly. She must have a thousand different scents of perfume and wear a different one every single day of the week, he reckoned. Every letter had seemed to radiate with the scent of a different flower, each one more beautiful to his sense than the last.

Hiram lowered himself down onto his makeshift bed of linens and blankets and rugs, then turned the envelope in his hands and inspected the front of it. It was a thick yellow parchment of quality stock. He wondered if perhaps her father was not in the business of trading such goods because like the scents, each letter seemed to arrive in a different type and weight of stationary. He'd have never believed it if you had told him that so many different kinds of paper even existed in the entire world.

What remained constant though was Clara's beautiful, flowing hand. She began each word with a capitalized letter and each capitalized letter including big circular scrolls within their construction. Even before he read anything, he liked to just look at the whole of her letters and admire the letters. Truly, she was more than a writer of letters. She was an artist of sorts and he was certainly her greatest admirer.

Gingerly, Hiram removed the matching parchment from its snug home inside of the envelope. As if handling the most delicate robin's egg or tiniest flower observed in nature, he unfolded the single page and read her words to him.

December 22nd, 1869

My Dearest Hiram,

It Has Been So Long Since We Have Seen One Another. I Can Only Hope That You Still Remember My Face After All Of The Months That Have Gone By. Christmas Is In Full Season Here And The Joy Of My Family Is In Full Bloom.

But I Can Only Think Of You. I Remember Your Face, Hiram. It Is The Sweetest And Kindest Face That I Have Ever Known. And Even With So Much Happiness Around Me, I Can Only Think Of You And Sadly Yearn For A Time That We Shall Be Together Once More. I Pray That This Shall Be The Final Christmas That We Do Not Spend In The Company Of One Another. Papa Says That All Is Still As Planned And We Shall Be Moving On To Nebraska This Summer My Love. How Slowly These Days Pass Now That We Shall Be Together At Last! I Can Scarcely Control My Elation At The Marking Of Each Day And The Hour Of Our Reunion Grows Nearer.

Forever Yours in Love,

Clara Mary Smith

Hiram released a deep breath and smelled the flowery fragrance once more inside of the envelope. "I love you Clara," he said, and then just as gingerly as he had removed it, he folded it and slid it neatly back inside. Next, he tucked the entire thing back into his coat pocket and hooked the small lip of the bottom side of the plank that kept hidden his treasures. Behind the plank on the horizontal board that served as his shelf, Hiram removed the tin and placed the envelope inside with the others.

There were 17 such envelopes inside of the tin now. How many more had been discovered and burned by his father over the years, he could never know. Likewise, how many letters of his own never made it into her hand could not be certain as her mother had been known to intercept their correspondence from time to time as well. Why it was that everyone could not simply leave them be was a mystery to him and one that he could not decipher. It was without reason to him that her mother and father had sought to keep them apart even in their youth in Illinois.

The two had been fast and inseparable friends during his time living with his aunt. And always, Clara was the one person that he had trusted, the one soul he could confide in and depend upon. More than even that, she was the one body in this world that he truly loved with all of his heart.

Hiram then removed another box from his shelf. This one was larger and flat. Placing it upon his lap as he sat back down, he unwound the string from the tiny button that held the box closed. Then he flipped the top up by its handmade leather hinges. The inside of the box wood still retained some of the original cigar labels of the several smaller boxes he had used to create the thing.

Closing the lid, he set upon the top a single sheet of paper, his ink well, and his pen, worn from thousands of words. It did not make for fancy writing those days. Having made the trip from Illinois and his recital days with a single worn tip, there were no sharp edges from which the ink could gently flow any longer. Rather, it simply let spill the ink along the bottom of its rounded metal at whatever place that it chose to flow. As the result he was forced to write larger letters than he would have liked and mindful of the space, he always left so much unsaid that he'd desired to convey to her.

Hiram looked thoughtfully at the blankness of the page before him. His parchment caused him to cringe at the coarseness of it compared to hers. He wished that he had a decent quill tip to write with so that she could see how much he cared for her. He wished that each word could appear in a way that she could see within it his love for her. He wished that he had better paper as well, the fancy sort with the colorful threading in it from fine clothe, instead of the thick, coarse stuff wrought directly from wood pulp. But alas, he had only what he had, and once again he would have to rely solely upon his few words to quell her over and keep her heart as his own. So it was that he began to write.

January 16, 1870

My Dear Clara,

You may rest well my love, for I could never forget the beauty of your face. It is within that face, those beautiful blue eyes, and your charming smile that all of my faith now lies. Every future hope, dream, and ambition of my life is with you and being with you. You are my beauty, my love, my sweet, my everything. Every breath I draw is in honor of you. Every beat of my aching heart marks only time lived in anticipation of being with you once more. I love you fully, completely, eternally.

Yours Forever,

Hiram Wilson

Hiram inspected his letter. He carefully reread each word three times to make certain there were no errors in his spelling. It didn't matter much really as it was his only piece of paper, but nonetheless, he wanted to make sure it was as good as he could do for the now.

Carefully, he made tiny marks along the edges of the paper using guide marks he had drawn on the lid of his writing box. In so doing, he would guarantee himself a perfect tri-folded letter each time. Hiram made his first fold then creased the edge with his finger, then did so again and inspected his work. The fold was slightly less than the perfect crease he had intended by his design and the leading edge of the thing stuck above the rest just slightly. It would have to be folded over itself to make the envelope, but still, there it was.

He addressed the envelope to Clara first then stuffed the letter inside of it. Next he lit the tiny candle that he kept inside of his box for just such occasions and dripped a dab of the colorful thick red wax on to the seam of the closed envelope. Then using a small metal bolt head, he pressed in his mark and sealed the thing for delivery. It was not much of a mark; just a square pressed into the dark red wax, but it was his still. For her part, Clara always used a bird stamp of some sort to seal her letters. That was yet another reason that Hiram insisted on opening them on the ends.

Finally, Hiram looked the thing over once more and tucked it neatly inside of his coat pocket. He was satisfied that it was as best it could be and ready to hand off for delivery to his Clara. Last, but definitely not least, he reached into the bottom of the box and pulled out his three cent nickel piece. It was the most difficult thing he'd had to come by each month to complete the cycle that maintained his sanity, but always, somehow, he managed to find a way. He had found that despite his good nature and religious upbringing at the hand of his aunt he was not wholly immune, nor ill affected, by even stooping so low as to pick his father's pockets once or thrice when he staggered in from a good drunk in town. Truly, he had never missed a cent of it either and probably, a just God would forgive such trespasses for the sake of love anyhow.

Hiding the nickel in his clutched hand, Hiram replaced the plank covering his stored treasures, and blew out the light of his lamp. Then out he went into the blinding light of the sunny winter day once more and into the cabin to join the two old friends. There he would await the opportunity to pass off his secret dispatch directly under the spying eyes and prying nose of his father. It was a dangerous mission to be certain, but throughout the entire civil war, not a more worthy cause for a dispatch had been witnessed. Neither had there been a more trustworthy courier to carry out such a job as the good Mr. Glenn either.

Besides, so long as Mr. Glenn was about, his old friend, Hiram's father, was certain to be in the best of moods and in fine behavior. He'd not lay a hand on his son with a witness about. God forbid that anyone knew the truth about the man. Suspect what they might, in old Elias' mind, he was still a respected man about the county. Hiram scoffed at the thought of it and stepped inside the cabin wearing a cheerful smile for them both.

Chapter 10   Life At Harris Inn

Evelyn had stitched until the morning was well along. She had really taken to staying at the Inn. Mrs. Harris, a widow of a well to do doctor, had turned her huge elaborate home into an Inn not for sustenance, but more or less, to fill the voids within the house and give her company. Mrs. Harris, however far along in her years she may have been, was accustomed to hard living and a lot of it, as well as always having folks around to care for.

Without children at home any longer, or grandchildren who lived nearby, or even a husband to tend to, she had found herself without meaning in her life. She had opened her home as an Inn under the auspice that a widow required the money, but truth was she didn't require a penny of it. She had known Evelyn before as well. She and her son, Ellis, were far from mere strangers. In fact, as parishioners of the same church, it was as if family had come to stay within her residence and she cared for them as if they were her own.

It was such a joy for the old woman to rise and make a breakfast for the boy especially. Ellis reminded her of her very own son when he was only 11. Evelyn had even become content enough to stay in her room during the hour prior to school and stitch, leaving Ellis and Mrs. Harris alone to their own devices. After breakfast, Mrs. Harris would even make the boy a lunch to take to school with him. For his part, Ellis loved the extra doting and attention. What's more, there was always some fresh baked surprise awaiting him in his lunch pail. Between Mrs. Harris' doting and Mr. Logan's fishing trips and the like, it seemed that Ellis was fast becoming the most popular young man in town. It was clear to everyone involved that the boy loved the attention.

Mrs. Harris' clock had just chimed nine in the morning when Evelyn finally emerged from her room and came down for breakfast. She was a very light eater as of a morning and she never had been able to eat too early in the day without it having ill effects on her stomach. Mrs. Harris, aware of the quirk, had insisted upon making her a special breakfast of her own long after all of the other guests had eaten and gone for the day.

"Good morning, Mrs. Harris," Evelyn smiled brightly as she walked into the kitchen behind the old woman who stood washing dishes in a tub. "Did Ellis cause you any mischief this morning?"

"Oh good heaven, no dear," Mrs. Harris turned and flashed a bright, warm smile to the much younger woman. "That boy is an absolute angel. I am so happy to have him about. This house has been too long without the likes of him here, Evelyn. And how are you this morning?"

"I am quite well, thank you," Evelyn replied. Mrs. Harris was such a genuinely happy soul and warm, kind spirit. Evelyn so much enjoyed her company, especially in the mornings. Her company was as if a bright sunny spring morning greeted you each and every single day regardless of the weather outside.

Evelyn believed that there was something quite welcoming about Mrs. Harris' smile. It was as if she had gone back in time when her very own grandmother was still alive. Indeed, Mrs. Harris even sported the same short, stout figure of her grandmother. It was the build of a healthy woman who had worked hard most of her life. So hard in fact that if she were to stop abruptly, she would probably falter and die.

It was the place of old women like Mrs. Harris, with long beautiful white hair kept neatly in a bun and apron seemingly sewed to the front of her every dress, to care for others. Evelyn hoped that one day she would be such a woman, caring for others and cooking delightful treats for children. It was such a peaceful and happy existence the old woman seemed to live, so comfortable in her aging skin, and always offering that same sense of comfort, her learned wisdom and fresh baked cookies to all those who entered her kitchen.

"What mischief are you to seek on this fine day, Evelyn?" Mrs. Harris asked, as she turned from her washing and poured them both a fresh cup of coffee.

"Well," Evelyn replied thoughtfully, blowing the steam that rose from the top of her cup. Mrs. Harris' coffee was so delightful. Usually Evelyn had preferred to take a tea instead, but Mrs. Harris used a special bean in her mix that produced a light, hearty flavor that Evelyn simply adored. "I am running low on my hues of red threads, so I shall have to go out and procure some new ones for starters. Would you care to join me, Mrs. Harris?"

"No thank you," Mrs. Harris smiled, "I have far too much work to do here it would seem."

"Mrs. Harris, you work too much. You should come with me and enjoy the fruits of your labors for once. It looks to be a glorious day," Evelyn said, sipping from her coffee cup.

"No thank you dear," Mrs. Harris replied politely, "I would only slow you down I'm afraid. Besides, I am all the more comfortable here during the winter months these days."

"Suit yourself then, but the offer is always there for you," Evelyn said. "I cannot thank you enough for how you have taken on with Ellis, and cared for us both."

"It is I who should be thanking the two of you," said Mrs. Harris. "The two of you have brought a life into this house that it has not known in many years. I do hope that you will stay on and enjoy the summer in the yard and the garden here with me. It is most wonderful here in the summer. Have you heard from your family?"

"Well, as a matter of fact, yes I have. Only yesterday I received a dispatch from mother and it would seem that your wish may well be made true. They have moved up the time when they are coming here to July. So I shall, in all probability, wait here for them to arrive instead of running off to Illinois," Evelyn said, fixing the pleats of her dress.

"That is wonderful news dear," replied Mrs. Harris. "That makes me so happy to hear of it. And if it becomes a burden to you to pay for your stay here then think nothing of it."

"That is very kind of you. You are such a fine woman," Evelyn said, sinking in her chair a bit and cocking her head slightly with a tiny smile on her lovely face. "That means so much to me, really it does. But Mr. Bates left us very comfortably suited and I should have no troubles paying you for our entire stay through July. Come that time we shall either become more permanent residents of the county or be moving on to greener pastures with my mother."

"So, you are still dallying with your decision about Mr. Logan then I gather?" Mrs. Harris regretted having said it even as it had passed over her lips. It had never been in her nature to gossip or pry and she immediately became flush with embarrassment at her breach of manners. "I'm sorry Evelyn, dear. That is none of my affair. It is only that you are becoming as a daughter to me and, well...I am just sorry."

Evelyn was admittedly taken aback by the comment. She had no idea that her intentions, or lack thereof, with Jasper Logan had become so well known. "Think nothing of it Mrs. Harris. There is no reason to apologize. I simply was not aware that we have become a talk of the town."

"Nonsense dear," Mrs. Harris replied. "No one is talking about anyone that I am aware of. It is only that he has come to call on you and Ellis so often here that I had assumed. You are both such beautiful young people. I assumed too much. Please dear, think nothing of the babblings of an old woman."

"No," Evelyn replied, sensing the sincerity in the old woman's apology. "I am sorry Mrs. Harris. We need not have any secrets between us and I feel the same about you. I am sorry that I have not spoken of it with you before now. Besides, the good Lord only knows that I could use the counsel and advice. Mr. Logan is indeed pursuing the course that I should stay on here and remarry. And he is of the type of gentleman that a woman would desire to marry *if* she had that desire."

"But you don't want to remarry yet so soon after losing your husband?" Mrs. Harris sat up straighter in her chair. She was still no gossip and would never share their talks with anyone, but that did not mean that she did not enjoy hearing such familiar conversation.

"No, that isn't it at all," confided Evelyn. "Jasper is very successful and handsome and he has been so good to us since Mr. Bates passed last year. I honestly do not know what I would have done without him."

"Then what is it dear?" Mrs. Harris looked genuinely puzzled. If she herself were only thirty or forty years the younger, she'd be right in line with every single woman in the county trying to catch the eye of the man that Evelyn was now considering *not* marrying.

"There is just something about his character that I have yet to decide upon," Evelyn replied.

"What about his character bothers you?" Mrs. Harris queried.

"I don't know," said Evelyn, swirling the coffee in the bottom of her cup.

"Well then, say no more love," Mrs. Harris said softly, pouring her another cup. "Jasper Logan may well be the most respected and successful young business man in the county, but no one can know what is truly in his heart but you. A woman has a way of just *knowing* things like that. So, you learn what it is you need to learn about the man first and never question or doubt for a second, your own intuition."

Evelyn set down her cup and rose from her chair. Mrs. Harris was still standing holding the coffee pot in her hand and turned to set it back atop the stove. To the old woman's surprise, as she turned, Evelyn grabbed her and pulled her in close, giving her a big, warm hug. It was not the sort of hug that women tended to give to one another as a greeting either. But rather, it was the familiar deep, strong hug of a mother and a daughter. Mrs. Harris loved it so much that she thought she might be drawn to tears even before Evelyn began to speak to her.

"Mrs. Harris," Evelyn said softly in her ear while continuing to hold her tight. "Thank you so much for that. You have no idea how much I needed to hear that very thing. I cannot begin to tell you how much you have come to mean to me. Thank you so much."

By the time Evelyn had let her go and the women stepped back from one another both of them had been reduced to joyful tears. Both of them understood what it meant to be a woman and a widow. Then, after that day, they would share something even deeper. For so many women would know the pain of loss, of husbands and children alike. Few however, would ever break the restraints of polite society to gain a real sister in the world in 1870.

Mrs. Harris would change her mind and the two of them would go about the merchants on the town square for the better part of the day. It was a wonderful day for them both. By the time it would end, they would have shared nearly everything that a woman might with another woman. Truly, despite the differences in age or all else, they had become sisters by nightfall and Mrs. Harris would dote over Ellis all the more because of it.

Chapter 11   Logan's Creamery

Jasper Logan had made it into the creamery even earlier that morning. He had not expected to see Jacob Lyman in quite as early as himself, yet there he was arriving at the very same minute. The two of them walked inside together.

The building itself still had the smell of fresh cut wood, having not quite settled upon her foundations before the butchery addition was begun. Adding to the pleasantries of the aromas about them were a variety of other things like the sawdust kept fresh upon the floors throughout the building that arrived from the lumber mill each afternoon. Then there was the cheese room where the smells of aging cheeses wafted out into the main building growing thicker as a man walked through the presses with their large wooden crank handles and shiny iron gears. They allowed a single man or boy to exert a thousand pounds of pressure to press a scoop of curds into a wheel of cheese.

Even before the men had arrived, the drivers of the teams had been behind the building waiting. On their wagons the copper

75

tanks overflowing with fresh milk had recently arrived with the freshly extracted morning milk. This was Logan's way. Always, he insisted upon having the milk brought directly to the building as fresh as could be with no other storage or vessels used between cow and creamery. He believed that it was the variety of wooden kegs and glass and metal jugs of every sort that caused the bitterness of most other dairies.

Jasper Logan would have none of it. Any container with his name upon it would be fresh and free of the contaminants that marked most dairy operations of any size of the day. To that very end, he had himself designed and manufactured large wagon vessels of copper that could be hauled directly inside of the creamery then hoisted off and set into place to begin the cream rendering or siphoned off to another process. The empty vessels from the day before, having been thoroughly scrubbed and cleaned could then be loaded on the wagon and drawn back to the farm to be filled once more that afternoon.

"Good morning to you, Jacob!" said Jasper cheerfully.

"Good morning, Mr. Logan," Jacob replied, tipping his hat a bit as they entered the building.

That's one of the things that he truly admired about Mr. Logan. He spoke to every man on his floor each day. The other thing Jacob liked was that he was a man unafraid to dirty his own hands. Mr. Logan was not like the bankers or other wealthy men in town who hid in their office while other men toiled to make them richer. No, Mr. Logan was out amongst the worst of it with his men.

The two crossed the central lane of the large building and slid open the doors that allowed the two wagon drivers to enter. Each of them ran a team of mules whose droppings must be cleared straight away when they pulled out. It was just another quality assurance of Mr. Logan's. He was almost crazy with worry about anything that might give a foul odor and impart it into the cheeses especially.

"Cheeses are like newborn infants", Logan would say to his men, "when first pressed they are each one of them susceptible to everything poor of nature in their environments. It is to us to protect them at all costs."

This he adhered to, even to go so far as to forbid the smoking of pipes inside of his building. No one had ever heard of such a thing in all of Lucas County before either; no smoking of pipes to protect a cheese, of all things!

Closing the doors, Jacob walked back through the building as the drivers hooked on their loads. He opened the doors of the mighty burner as he had done a hundred times and stoked the coals inside with a long steel rod until the flames lapped up the sides. Then he began carrying armloads of wood stacked alongside the tanks upon the wagons and throwing them inside. The burner was nothing more than an oversized wood-stove, but it was nearly as tall as two men and just as wide and held enough wood to keep it burning controlled for days on end with a full load. Trouble was no one could ever get a full load into it because of the size of the thing. Anyway, it was just as easy to load it once a day. They had discovered over time that by bringing just what could fit in the wagons along-side the milk tanks that it was more than enough to keep the fires burning consistently until the following morning. It also was beneficial in that they did not require a store of wood inside the building for rats and mice and bugs to call their homes.

Jacob finished loading the wood and pushed the heavy doors closed on the burner. Then he hurried over to help the driver of the second wagon who was having trouble getting the swing arm to turn with the heavy tank of milk on it. Jasper noticed him hurrying and saw the driver struggling and the two of them arrived to give the tank a push in unison. The driver thanked them both and lowered the tank into position on the custom made base.

As they completed the loading of the empties, Jacob slid open the large front doors to let the wagon drivers pass back out. As the wagon drivers let loose their breaks and their mules began to trudge forward out the door, some of the other workers of the creamery began arriving. Jacob closed the doors and Mr. Logan said hello to a few more men before walking away toward the wooden steps that led up to an elevated platform overlooking the entire creamery. Perched up along an entire side of the enormous building, the walkway ran the length of it. All along the walkway were doors leading into the creamery offices where the accountant, the filer, the seller, and Mr. Logan himself were located.

Logan walked along the catwalk and stopped in front of the door that led into his office. He grasped the door handle and then paused thoughtfully. Hat in hand, his thick black hair flipped upwards as he spun around quickly on the heel of his boots and looked down upon his creamery at Jacob Lyman. He was so young, that one, and yet...

"Jacob!" Mr. Logan called out and his voice echoed through the empty building.

Jacob looked up from shoveling the manure that the mules had left behind.

"Yes sir?" he called.

"Leave that and come to my office. Mr. Hansen will finish cleaning that floor. Mr. Hansen," Logan said, looking down to a man who had just walked in.

It was actually part of Hansen's duty anyhow, but the man was always arriving too late to tend to it properly. He was a shirker, that Hansen was, and everyone in the creamery knew it. He'd come in late as of a morning once he knew full well that the younger man would have the manure all shoveled and the floor polished in the mule's wake before Mr. Logan had arrived. For the past year Mr. Logan had been keeping himself busy tending to the affairs of Evelyn Bates' farm in the mornings. Just then, it seemed that he was arriving as he had before. Hansen nodded his head and went about shoveling the piles of manure where Jacob had left off. It was a suitable job for Hansen too.

Jacob had never been upon the catwalk above the plant. He'd never had any call to be up there. The only time a man ever really did go up there aside from the foremen, it meant that they were being fired or at least having their skin ate off by Mr. Logan. Jacob removed his hat and clutched it tightly in his fists as he ascended the stairs. His heart sank as he made his way along the walkway. Jacob even had to rest a hand upon the wooden railing as he walked to steady himself. Between the height and his nerves, it seemed as though he was growing dizzier with each step. He wondered what he would tell his Mother or how in the world he would break it to his father that he had brought this shame upon their family. He knew he was about to be fired. Sullenly, he turned and followed the elder man into his office.

Jasper Logan opened the curtain on his office windows and the morning light flooded inside of the room. He had one window that looked over the creamery and another that had been built into the side of the building like a dormer. With the whitewash painted walls a light creamy color, it took the light well and shone as the beams of sun bounced to and fro inside the office.

"Have a seat," Logan said to the young man, waving his hand toward a chair as he passed around a desk and sat down himself.

"Thank you, Sir," Jacob replied nervously, feeling the sweat begin to trickle down his armpits. Nerves had always afflicted him so. Once, he set about to kiss one of the notoriously beautiful Beatty Sisters and even before he got close enough to her to get slapped, he had sweat dumping out of him from every orifice...and it was only February!

"I was called upon by Mr. Mason last evening," Logan said firmly.

Jacob swallowed hard. It wasn't going to be good. Mr. Mason was the cheese foreman and the man hated Jacob. He had intended to hire on his own son-in-law to the position that Jacob had filled. But it was against policy of Mr. Logan's and not in line with his desire to hire individuals from prominent families within the community. But ever since he had started working there, Mr. Mason had ridden him and treated Jacob as a foundered horse, calling him good for nothing and the like.

"...and it is my sad duty to inform you that he has returned to Ohio country on the news of a loss in his family," Logan continued. "I employ some twenty-six men at this creamery Jacob, plus two mule drivers, plus another fifteen milkers at my own farm. But, of the twenty-six that I employ directly here, can you explain to me how it is that you are always the first one here as of a morning and the last one to leave in the evening?"

"Sir," Jacob was taken aback and through his nervousness he could not tell whether to trust the sincerity of the man's voice, or the oddity of his words. "I don't understand sir," he replied.

"Mr. Mason will not be coming back, Jacob. And I would like you to take his place as the foreman of the cheese rooms. You'd answer directly to Superintendent Mills and then myself of course. I'm certain that you know how important that area is to me and what a responsibility that job is?"

"Oh, yes sir. Yes sir, I do!" Jacob said, still reeling from the transition from nervous fear to nervous elation. "You will not be sorry, sir."

"Good," Logan said, eyeing the young man carefully. "Hard work and commitment should not be without reward in this world. None have learned faster or have worked harder than you have. Do this job well and you may expect to be superintendent of the works one day when Mr. Mills retires or moves along. I shall give you a week to learn the job and if Mr. Mills is in approval, we shall see to it that you receive an extra half share of the facility," he said.

"I don't know what to say, Mr. Logan," Jacob replied. "I am honored that you have chosen me sir. You needn't worry about a thing."

"Excellent. That's quite well Jacob," Logan said, smiling at him, "because I am counting on you." And with that he rose and shook the young man's hand.

Jacob thanked him once more before departing the office. He no longer required the steadiness of the handrail either. His feet seemed to glide across the boards. He paused only for half a second and looked out upon the vast expanses of the creamery. The groups of men were still shuffling in and Hansen had finished polishing the floor in the central lane. With the first taste of success fresh upon his lips, Jacob was filled with elation and something else that he had not known well before that day; ambition. It was true unbridled ambition, not to be confused with whimsical fantasy or dreaming of things unat-

81

tainable. Yes, he had thought to himself looking out upon the creamery floor, it would be his one day. By God, it *would* really all be his!

Chapter 12   Spring 1870

Spring, it seemed, had bloomed early in Missouri in 1870. By the end of March, a run of unseasonably warm days lasting two weeks had caused all of the snow to melt. With the exceptions of the marshy bottoms, the ground had dried itself in the warming sun and the blowing of a light southerly wind. It was a welcome and stark change from the blizzards and terrible winters of the previous several years which had seemed without end.

The weather brought so much cheer to the men and the animals alike that even Elias Wilson himself had been wrought kinder during those weeks. So much so, in fact, that he allowed Hiram to take on a job helping an aging neighbor with his chores. The agreement was that Hiram was to tend to his own chores at home first and then he could walk the two miles to Mr. Damm's house and do as he saw fit. It went without saying, but was said anyways, that Hiram would be expected to give any wages received to his father, "for his keep."

Of course, this presented Hiram with the opportunity to begin to squirrel away some pay to use for the coming day when he and Clara would finally steal away together and marry. Richard Damm had only a few years prior been a successful and happy farmer with three sons and a wife. The cholera had come to his farm in 1866 though, and he was the only one who remained in its wake.

Even despite it all, Mr. Damm had remained a kind soul. He must have been a very happy spirit before losing his family because as he spoke even then, Hiram could see a smile in his eyes. He was not a man accustomed to having paid help either. What he had, he'd cleared and planted with his own hands once. As he had aged, his sons had begun to fill in where they were needed. It was only then that he had finally admitted defeat to his advancing years and sought help in his daily work, recognizing that he could no longer do it all alone. What's worse, his fields had been suffering as the result of his vein efforts to stay atop it all.

Hiram had withheld it from Mr. Damm that he would be abruptly departing in late July. He felt ill of himself for doing it too. He had correctly figured though, that the aging man would simply let him go and find another boy right away to begin working with prior to the harvest.

All day as Hiram worked, his mind raced with the excitement of the coming adventure and his heart ached for Clara. Hiram knew precious little about the ways of the world or what they would do to sustain themselves. He only knew that more than anything he had ever dreamed of, he *needed* to be with her. It was as if the very thought of *not* being with her stole away his very will to breathe. In the grand scheme of human history, man has sought to provide himself with the necessities of life in food and water, followed by shelter and clothing. For Hiram though, the list of such necessities was extended by one; Clara. For him, she was the first necessity of life. So long as he had her by his side, he reckoned that the rest would fall into their proper place as the result of hard work. Without her there however, he would most certainly die of a different kind of starvation, another sort of neglect.

All throughout his time at his Aunt's house in Illinois, Clara had been his only friend. As small children they had spent their lives intertwined by their adjoining back yard. The harsh realities of the world around them could not penetrate their secret world together where every chicken coop was a castle, every walnut grove a forest filled with adventure.

Clara had been the only person he'd ever known who he could really talk to about anything at all. As a child, it had been her that had consoled him through the loss of his mother. She was the only soul who'd ever discussed it with him, or who had ever listened to him weep and let it be so. As they grew, he'd only just begun to realize that his feelings ran deeper than merely friends. It was only when he was moved away, back to his father's farm, when he realized that he had no desire to so much as think of living without her.

Hiram had tried to talk to other girls on the rare Saturdays when they had gone to town, but in the end he found them to be useless. Even the few who had shown any interest in him were rejected as prospects for one reason or another. He had originally thought that it was because their hair was too short or their conversation lacked one thing or the other. In the end however, he had come to understand that he had no use for any of them simply because they were not *her*. They were not, in one way or another, Clara. In the end he had concluded that she was the only one who could tame his heart. Indeed, she had laid claim to it years before when he was only a small boy and it belonged in its entirety to her and her alone.

Between the long walks to and from Mr. Damm's farm, and while he labored his hours away on both spreads, Hiram's thoughts were filled with visions of Clara. At times, he would think of her and miss her so much that he would begin to sob from the aching sadness that dwelt within his heart. Other times, the memory of her soft voice caused him to smile uncontrollably while he worked away. Still other times yet, he could think of her and remember the words she had placed so beautifully upon the fancy colored parchments of her letters. During those times, it was as if he would awaken suddenly from an already waking dream to discover tears of blissful joy streaming down his cheeks.

No matter the course of Hiram's thoughts, his work remained hard and steady. Through his labor, he had figured, each shovel of manure, each rake full of hay, drew him yet closer to Clara. Mr. Damm could not help but be impressed by the boy's efforts. For his part, Mr. Damm even began to think of clearing again, of razing more scrub ground and breaking open new fields for harvest. When he had first come this part of the country, he'd been young and with the might of his own arms, had cleared the timber, and pulled the stumps, and plowed the virgin soil. There was something about being in the presence of youthful vigor that made the older man begin to feel his own oats once more himself.

It would be in the midst of such exuberance that Mr. Damm would even give Hiram a modest increase in his wage. The increase had the desired effect too, for Hiram seemed to dig even harder after that. The older man though, could have no way of knowing that Hiram did so, not out of gratitude or general ambition. Instead, the extra pennies would be safely tucked away in a tin, hidden behind a section of wall, and applied toward the imagined expense of an approaching wedding day.

As if the God's themselves had smiled down upon him approvingly, Hiram would have yet another bout of good fortune that very evening. Arriving home well after dark, he found the place to be barren of life, his father gone to town no doubt, to cast about with the other drunks for the night. Hiram knew full well that whenever he wasn't home before dark that there was little chance of his returning any time soon. In fact, *if* the old man did manage to stumble home before dawn, and that was questionable at best, then you could rest assured that it would be closer to the rising of the next sun than the setting of the last.

Hiram set about inside the cabin to make himself something to eat. After which, he would retire to his private quarters in the wood shed. There was no sense in having another night's rest disturbed by a mean drunk rolling in and rousing him from his bed inside of the house. He was far too tired for any such nonsense.

Hiram reached above him and, striking a match, set flame to the lantern in the kitchen. As he turned the wick up, the flickering light filled the room with dancing shadows. As the flickering subsided and he slipped down the glass cover over it, the light settled in and cast a dim, yet steady glow throughout the small room.

Turning his efforts toward the stove, something on the table caught the attention of his weary eyes. His heart raced with excitement. It was a letter from Clara! It lay there in full view of the world, unmolested. There could only be one explanation for it. It was as if divine intervention had stepped in to see his father off early on a drunk that day. Mr. Glenn must have slipped inside as always, and finding the place empty, set the letter haphazardly upon the kitchen table. Hiram wondered how many such letters had been cast into the fire of the stove by his father as he quickly tucked the treasure inside of his shirt.

The hunger from a long day's labor and miles of walking subsided just then. For far more powerful than his own empty stomach was the aching in his heart for Clara. Hiram reached above him and turned down the lantern wick, allowing the tiny house to fade to darkness once more. With his hands he made his way out the door and with his treasure secure, he tucked himself away inside of the wood shed.

With the door secured by an inside latch of his own making, Hiram lit his own lantern and then went about his routine of prying the board away from the wall, then settling in to open the letter and smell inside and respond to it. He'd not had one since January of that year and the weeks that passed had seemed eternal.

As much as every day with thoughts of Clara were a gift, they also brought with them a dark, haunting fear that only another letter could give cause to ease. For even as much as they had promised devotion to one another, there always remained within his chest the fear that she might stray and find another, or that her heart would simply change its course for him. The mere thought of it was almost more than he could bear. It came on like a plague upon his stomach and grew as if a cancer upon his innards. The only cure for all that ailed him was her letters. As he cut open the end of the latest, a tear trickled down his cheek at the thought of losing the only thing that he held dear in this world and the next.

March 12, 1870

My Dearest Hiram,

Once Again My Letter Remained Unanswered Last Month. I Can Only Pray That You Have Not Lost Hope In Me My Love. I Hope That It Was Only The Acts Of Some Negligent Post Master. How I Wish That We Were Together Already.

Our Reunion Cannot Come Soon Enough. Indeed, Our Plans For July Are Still For The Last Of It. We Shall Pass On Our Journey Through Lucas County In Iowa To Call Upon One Of Our Lot, So All Should Remain As Planned.

My Heart Cannot Beat Without You Near Me For Much Longer I Fear. How Much I Have Grown To Love You. For As Much As My Breast Requires Air To Breathe My Heart Needs Thee.

Yours In Eternal Love,

Clara Mary Smith

The next morning, as Hiram roused to the growling of a beast within his stomach, he would find his empty lantern swinging above his head and the crumpled page of fine parchment clutched firmly within his hand. That night, he had dreamed of her again.

He dreamt of a grand feast of the likes of which he had never before known. There were hams and fowl and every sort of the freshest vegetables that a body could imagine all along the breadth of a long, beautiful, well carved table. On each side of the table there were children, handsome children, sitting calmly and patiently, all smiling up at him as he approached.

Taking his place at the table he bowed his head to say a prayer. When he raised it again he saw Clara at the farthest end of the table smiling back at him. The table seemed to go on forever and the children along both sides were numerous beyond counting. Yet, for as distant as she was from him, he had never felt closer to her. The two of them were inseparably linked beyond imagining by each of the children that filled the expanse between them.

It was a glorious and wonderful dream.

March 27, 1870

My Darling Clara,

Last night I dreamt of you once more my love. We had a table full of beautiful children and a bountiful feast among us. Sure as the sun shall rise in the morning, we shall soon be together. I know little, but this I know with all of my heart. I am earning keep and pay for us now my love. Fear not, for very soon we shall be as one. My love for you only grows stronger with each day. It must be so, as if it had been divined by the Gods themselves.

Your Love Always,
Hiram Wilson

Chapter 13   Blood Milk

Gaylord Lyman had awoken the same as so many mornings, to the God awful smells. He would do without much sleep that night having come in very late. Word had arrived through the Anti Horse Thief Society that there had been a number of vagabonds who had ridden up from Missouri to the East the day before. They had stolen some horses somewhere south of Ottumwa and had been rumored to be following the Mormon Trace road heading west. The sheriff, along with several business men and farmers, had assembled to head them off should they attempt to ride into Lucas County.

The result, as so many times before, was a lot of good people losing a great deal of sleep. There had been some excitement however, when two unsuspecting travelers had been captured and taken in. Fortunately, they had gone in peacefully to town at gunpoint, but the sheriff knew all too well how things might have ended.

It was his greatest fear about the Anti Horse Thief Society. Once, they had been a necessity to ward off the bands of outlaws coming up through Missouri before and during the war, but now he was beginning to view them as more of a threat than anything else. They were no threat to the community itself, because to a man, they were each the best of them, but he could not shake the feeling that eventually their eagerness would backfire upon them somehow.

It was only a matter of luck that the two cowboys they had stumbled upon that night had not put up a fight. What could they assume being met by a group of men with their guns drawn? They had been lucky alright, but luck alone only holds water for so long a time.

The sheriff shuffled into the kitchen and followed his routine of stoking the morning fire and starting the thick coffee that would see him through the day. As he had only begun his first cup, Sol entered the room and found his seat at the table. Shortly thereafter, Jacob followed.

"Will you finish telling us *now,* Pa?" Sol asked after brief morning greetings had been exchanged and both of the boys had found the coffee.

Jacob had not inquired again of the story. Gaylord had always admired those two traits in his eldest son; he rarely had allowed his curiosity to get the better of him, and his veins coursed with a patience even his own father, who was widely admired for the trait, had come to envy. Sol, had neither such trait and had questioned his father of the matter on at least a dozen occasions, but always, there was someone else present, or Jacob had not been about. Each time, Gaylord had insisted that it was a most private affair, but also one that he would endure the telling of only once.

Sheriff Lyman sighed and at first he looked impatiently at Sol to put him off once more. As he did, his mood was altered and he settled in to talk with his sons. He did not talk to them enough, he knew, and it had become all too easy to put the thing off, especially knowing that all too soon, that fall, he would be finished with his work as the County Sheriff, and have time enough to spend with them. But still, he was nagged by the acknowledgement that in this world, tomorrow does not always arrive as it had been planned, and for some it never comes at all.

"Where did I leave off?" he feigned the tiny hint of a smile at Sol to show that he was relenting amicably to the boy's persistence.

"You had drunk too much and woke up to some awful smell," Jacob chimed in. With all of his patience, the sheriff could still hear the eagerness in his voice.

"Ah," the sheriff replied, taking another big drink of his steaming coffee.

"There was that terrible smell all about that drove me upright. Sitting up, I opened my eyes and screamed in horror at what lay about me. There, in the middle of the prairie, amongst a vast ocean of sand and scrub that seemingly went on forever, was what appeared to be a red pond in the middle of it all. For so stained was the ground around us with blood that the entire area was a bright hue of dark, rich red that was by then drying in the early morning sun.

First, I thought myself dead or badly wounded as my body was awash in blood. I checked my limbs and my chest and felt my head, though, and I hadn't a scratch upon me. Standing up with my back to the fire pit, I could only stare at my hands in disbelief and wonder what had happened or if I wasn't the victim of some whiskey induced nightmare.

Then I turned and saw them. The rest of my party, Lieutenant Richards had been stripped of his clothes except his underwear. His legs and arms had been flayed wide open as if they had aimed to butcher him but got interrupted in the process. The other men were laid out similarly up a small sand hill. These, you could see, had been slaughtered near the fire, then dragged up the hill a bit as if a giant hand had been using them as playthings before depositing their mutilated corpses a little further on. But then I could see the small trails and I knew that they had been mortally wounded near the fire, and then allowed to crawl on their own accords up the hill like a cat might watch an injured mouse crawl in the belief that it might escape, only to cruelly deliver the death blows to it when he least expected it.

The horses and all of our gear and supplies were gone as well; all of it. Everything that we had to sustain us had been taken. Only the two pack mules were left behind, cut open to bleed out and die in the same ring of blood red stench and horror that I myself had awakened in.

It's easy to see now of course, but when you wake up in the middle of something like that it is as if your mind ceases to function properly. Everything was so confusing. I really had no idea what could have happened. My mind struggled to make heads or tails out of it all. And then I saw them.

About a mile off, just standing there on the horizon were six Indians on horseback, with extra horses, our horses, in tow. And then it was as if fireworks went off in my brain all at once. I saw it all very clearly and I knew it was them that had done it. Yet, here I was alive and there they were, just sitting there on their horses staring at me.

It was the most terrifying moment of my life. I scanned the area for a gun, for water, for anything. There was nothing to be found though; only the mutilated corpses, the thickening stench of drying blood and flesh, and thousands of flies. Then, when I looked back at the horizon, the Indians, who were still in the exact same positions and grouping as they had been only a moment before, had seemingly moved closer.

Time and looking back says that they hadn't moved at all. But the fear and the terror in my heart at that moment said that they had moved closer, inching toward me from the distant horizon. Panic struck, I turned and ran. I ran with all of my might back in the direction from which we had come. I ran further and faster than I have ever done before or since. And when my body could run no further I walked, but always, I kept moving.

Late that first evening, I stopped and sat upon a rock out there to rest. I had not looked behind me that day. I could not look behind me. It was too horrible to think that at any moment they could all come riding up and murder me. I knew that if I looked behind me that they would be there, closing in on me, hatchets in their murderous hands. But as I rested on that rock, I turned and looked behind me. Countless hours and miles had been put between us, and yet, there they were, that same group on horseback at about the same distance from me.

I still could not tell whether they were Sioux or Pawnee or Cheyenne. And I could not figure as to why they were waiting to kill me. Whatever the reasoning though, terror drove me from that rock after only a few seconds had passed. It was the last time that I would rest for days too.

I tried to stop on the second night, and they came in closer when I did and made camp. They took turns sneaking in closer yet and making all sorts of noises to try and scare me, and believe me, it worked. After a little less than an hour I started off again, walking toward safety and away from *them.*"

Jacob and Sol sat upon the edge of their chair. Their eyes were trained upon the lips of their father as he formed each new syllable. Their minds painted a vivid picture to the scene as each new word added details to it. So mesmerized had they become by their father that neither of them even noticed when he ceased speaking altogether. They merely sat, mouths agape, narrowly focused upon his lip.

They emerged from their dreams only when their minds could not link his next words to the rest of the story; when it ceased to make any sense.

"Good morning Alton," Gaylord said, smiling at his youngest son.

"Morning Papa," Alton replied, rubbing the sleep from his ten year old eyes and smiling through a tired morning haze.

"What brings you up at this hour?" The sheriff asked, messing his son's head of bleach blonde hair.

"I heard voices, Papa, and I wanted to see you," the boy replied.

The sheriff smiled warmly and drew him upon his lap. "And thus concludes our story for today boys," he said, smiling into the eyes of the older two, who had already begun to stir.

"I'm off to the creamery then, Pa," Jacob said as he rose from his seat.

"Dang it," Sol said, smiling at his own defeat, "just when it was getting good!"

Sheriff Lyman laughed aloud at him a bit, then turned his attentions to Alton and began bouncing him upon his knee. As much as he felt bad for not having the time for the older two boys, he was haunted most by his relations with his youngest son. There were entire stretches of days that often spread over the course of a week when he might not even see Alton at all.

Indeed, it was as if the two were strangers at times. It was for him and the mistakes he had made by not being around for the older boys that he was going to hang up his guns and turn in his badge that autumn. He had a lot of making up to do and he aimed to get started to doing it.

Jacob swilled down his coffee and walked out the door even before his mother had risen. His responsibilities at Logan's Creamery were consuming more of his time those days than ever before. Since he'd been placed in the charge of the cheese department, the young man had proven himself to be a real asset to Jasper Logan, and Jacob was determined to do everything that a body might to keep things that way.

On his short walk into town to the creamery that morning, Jacob could not help but imagine what it must have been like to be his father, so far from home in Indian country. His father had not only gone out onto the unknown of the frontier that was the far reaches of the Nebraska Territory at the time, but he had gone even beyond those boundaries into un-chartered lands. Jacob wondered if he himself would have had the courage to have gone on such a mission.

Passing the old city lake, he looked at the rippling waters as the wind passed gently over the top of them and wondered what it must have been like to be without that most basic of elements for so long a time. Jacob had seen difficult times when food was scarce, but he had never really gone without eating, and he had certainly *never* gone without water before, let alone done so with hostile Indians in full view. It was nearly unimaginable.

Opening the large overhead doors at the creamery, Jacob walked through the otherwise empty expanses of the building to let in the approaching teamsters with the morning's milk delivery. Like he had done so many times before, he closed the doors behind them and let in Mr. Hutchings and Mr. Bell.

Mr. Bell gave Jacob a loud and cheerful greeting as he passed while the former simply waved his hand quietly. Jacob began to remove the split wood from the wagon side. There was not nearly so much of it as before, for it was no longer required to warm the entire structure. Now, they would only burn as much and as long as it required to fire the boilers and build up steam to pressurize the flow lines throughout the building.

As he did so the stout Mr. Bell had climbed down from his rigging and began to struggle with the stubborn swing arm that held the full milk tank. Jacob could just see from the corner of his eye that the man was struggling with it again and yelled back to wait another moment and he'd come and help him. He had always like Mr. Bell as the man brought a bit of warmth in the mornings with the milk through his bright eyes and kind smile and jovial morning greetings.

There had been times during the worst of the winter that year when Mr. Bell had even stayed on for a while on his own hours to work with Jacob in the cheese room. He'd said that he needed to "warm his old bones" but really he only liked to visit some. Mr. Logan seemed to allow the practice as Mr. Bell was also working while he talked and it seemed to boost the productivity of all the men in the cheese room.

Jacob threw the last armload of wood into the burner and turned about just in the nick of time to hear the overhead swing boom begin to crack. He screamed at the top of his lungs for Mr. Bell to get out harm's way but it was too late.

The front door swung open and Mr. Logan walked in just as the entire structure supporting the full milk tank buckled and gave way. The tank crashed into the floor with a dull thud that shook the ground beneath Jacob's feet even as he was running toward the calamity. Slowly, the huge tank, with thousands of pounds of fresh morning milk, rolled off of the lifeless body of Mr. Bell and settled on to the hard packed earth, slowly emptying its contents on to the ground through a number of busted seams.

Jacob ran to Mr. Bell's side and knelt, but even he could see that there was no call to rush out for a doctor. Jasper Logan paused for a moment and then yelled for the men to help him. Jacob turned and was astonished to find that even as Mr. Bell's deformed and lifeless body lay there, Jasper Logan was rolling small barrels in place to catch the spilling milk lest it hit the ground. Jacob could only stand with his jaw agape and look on at the scene. It was surreal to him, as if in a dream that he could have never imagined having dreamt.

Even as Jasper Logan yelled for him to help once more, Jacob could only stand in awe and stare at him blankly. Then he quietly turned and walked out of the creamery door. As the other men filed slowly past arriving as of the morning, Jacob only stood there, grey skinned, wide eyed, and breathing heavily. Now, he too, had been marred by the smell of fresh blood in the morning and it was a sight and a smell that would never leave him. Fresh blood and fresh milk mingled together on the floor of the creamery and a man who he had come to look upon as a second father seemed oblivious to the former, yet scrambled to save only the latter of the two.

That morning, Jacob passed the city pond once again and looked across the water. Kneeling at its edge, he washed away the mixture of blood and milk that was beginning to dry on his hands. Stepping in, he even washed the concoction from his boots. But things like those, try as one might, can never be cleansed from a man's memory.

Jacob cupped his hands and let the cold, clear water run over his head. At the least, at the very least, it might not cleanse his entire soul, but the chill of the water as it passed down across his spine and on to his chest beneath his shirt, was a stark reminder that he was still alive. Standing, he drew a deep breath into his lungs and looked thankfully to the heavens for not making him seconds faster in his bid to have helped Mr. Bell push the swing arm that morning.

For a hundred mornings or more Jacob had loaded the burner and hurried to help the drivers with the stubborn swing arm. The men had cursed the thing incessantly, but Mr. Logan had only grumbled about the cost of replacing it when he would overhear them. It was a fairly new contraption, after all, and there seemed to be so many other things that they could see to first before replacing something that was still functional. It was difficult, yes, but still functional.

Thinking of it in those terms, Jacob thought that it had been only the cost of a new swing arm that had cost a man his life, and almost ended his own. Deep inside of his belly, like embers inside of a warm morning stove, an anger which he did not as of yet fully recognize or understand, began to grow. Jacob rose and trekked on down the path toward his family's farm uncertain if he would ever return to Logan's Creamery.

Chapter 14   Logan's Walk

Jasper Logan made the long walk through town to the Bell house south and west of the Chariton square several blocks. There, awaiting him in the yard was no less than three of Mr. Bells' small children. He smiled warmly at them as he unlatched the gate that kept the yard chickens and children alike secure and from straying. Removing his hat, he stepped up the rickety wooden steps and on to the porch.

Had he been buried yet, Mr. Bell would have been turning round within his grave to know that Jasper Logan had just walked upon the step that he had been meaning for months to replace. It had simply been one of those things that a man never quite seems to get around to doing, and now, Mr. Bell never would.

Mrs. Bell came to the door and greeted Mr. Logan with a reluctant smile as she wiped the flour from her hands on to her apron. She had never spoken directly to the man and propriety gave her pause to even so much as open the door to him without her husband being home. What an odd peculiarity it seemed for an employer to call upon a man's home when he himself was out at work. As he spoke through the screened door to her, the neighbors, some of whom had been watching suspiciously through their own windows as the scene unfolded, could hear the woman scream for several blocks.

Even as her screaming subsided, the church bells throughout the town began to toll for the kindly aging man, husband and father of six. Jasper Logan could only reach inside and hand the widow a small pouch containing some $80 in gold pieces. It was slightly in excess of a month's and a half wages for Mr. Bell, and there was no call for him to offer it to her, but it set his own mind at ease about the situation. At least it might help the woman get through these next few weeks and get her affairs in better order.

Still, Jasper Logan was at a loss for words. He turned away and left the consoling and comforting to the woman's friends and neighbors who he suspected might be better equipped to deal with that sort of thing. He'd never been very good at it really. Emotions were something that he had always believed better left to the weaker of the sexes. Such things can only blur a man's vision though, and cause him to make poor business decisions, he believed.

Walking away along the edge of the muddy road, Jasper looked at his boots and thought of the schematics at hand. He'd have to hire a replacement worker now. He would fill Mr. Bell's position with the aging Mr. Hamilton. Mr. Hamilton was growing too old to continue to serve him well in his current position on the farm anyhow. The teamster position would offer the aging worker a slightly better wage and an easier go of it. Most importantly, no one who had not proven themselves worthy of his trust would ever be allowed to haul his milk in to town. No, he'd just move Mr. Hamilton to the position and hire a man to replace him on the farm instead.

Then there was the issue of the replacement of the swing arm, and the mending of the tank to see to. The swing arm and rigging could be fixed by his own men as he employed more than one proficient carpenter among his men. The tank however, would be another matter. He would have to have it fixed by a skilled man from the city. But would it be of less expense to haul the thing there or have a man travel down with tools in tow? He'd have to see to it first thing in the morning.

Schematics. Costs. Such was the brutality of the world of business, he mused to himself. Even in light of the loss of human life, a business man must keep his head and hold all things into account. It was easy enough for a boy like Jacob Lyman to waiver in the shadow of such horror, but for a man like Jasper Logan, the world afforded him no such luxuries. Dozens of men and women earned their keep through his effort, and hundreds depended upon him for their daily sustenance.

The loss of Mr. Bell was a tragedy sure enough, but there was much more at stake than the comings and goings of just one man. If Jasper Logan himself had fallen that morning, he would have wanted his men to carry on in the same manner that he himself had done and see to it that his promise of fresh dairy was kept to the people of the Lucas County.

Jasper stopped alongside the city lake and gazed into the same waters as thoughtfully as Jacob Lyman had done earlier in the day. Logan's thoughts however were of a different ilk as he wondered if the thing might be spring fed and if so, how clean the water was at its source. Then he admired the wooded grove that lined the water's banks and wondered at what cost he might acquire such a property. There were a hundred good uses for the small lake, he'd reasoned, each of them far more lucrative than merely drawing ice from the surface. He made a note to himself to remember to inquire of it and then carried on along the wagon rutted dirt road that led west out of town.

Looking west across the vast meadow that spread out in front of him, Jasper could see the barn and lots that marked the Lyman residence. The first hints of green were coming on in the pastures and early calves could be seen frolicking along the bottoms while their mothers worked double time to try to collect the green shoots of grass that were only just beginning to emerge.

Crossing the bottoms, he had to skip from stone to stone to traverse the small creek that flowed across the surface of the valley that time of year. There was actually no creek there at all, but only a steady flow of water that passed through the grassy bottom only for a few weeks during the snow melt and the rains that were certain to follow. As the ground dried and was able to absorb more moisture, the water disappeared long before it reached the spot where the makeshift road crossed the bottom land.

Walking up the hill and on to the Lyman spread, Jasper admired the Sheriff's horses. For as much as Jasper took pride in his ability to breed fine milking cows, Sheriff Lyman was known for his horse flesh. Aside from his ability to select the finest, mellowest stock out of a thousand head, he also had a way with the animals that few in that part of the county could equal. One in particular caught Logan's eye and he thought that he might inquire of it on another day.

Opening the gate to the main yard, Jasper Logan entered and dogs began to rouse and bark. A figure emerged from the barn nearby and Jacob walked out into the sun to meet him.

"Hello Mr. Logan," Jacob hollered solemnly as he walked toward his employer.

"Good afternoon, Jacob," Jasper replied with a smile.

"I'm sorry that I left today, sir," Jacob said softly as his eyes turned toward his boots.

"Think nothing of it," Mr. Logan replied with every effort to appear only moderately cheerful.
"I went and paid a call on Mrs. Bell this afternoon."

"How is she?" Jacob inquired, swallowing hard and struggling to hold back tears.

"She is upset, of course," Mr. Logan replied, "just as we all are. Mr. Bell was a fine man, Jacob."

"Yes sir," Jacob replied. "He was."

"Listen," Jasper Logan reached out a hand and rest it upon the ball of Jacob's shoulder. "It must have been very difficult for you to see that today. And I know that you might not want to come back, but the fact is that I need you now even more than ever. You know, I was thinking as I walked here this afternoon about the responsibility that I have, that *we have*, to provide our service to this community. When that thing happened this morning all that I could think of was that Mr. Bell was gone, but we could still save the milk and make sure that no one would have to go without."

"I just..." Jacob struggled to find words to express what he felt.

"Now, hang on son," Mr. Logan said tersely, cutting him off. "I'm not finished. It may have appeared pretty callous of me to worry after the milk with a man lying there dead. But when I opened that creamery, I went around and asked hundreds of families to let me provide for them. Folks sold their cows because of me and that promise. My first responsibility, ours Jacob, is to ensure that we keep that promise. Now, are you going to be there in the morning to help me keep that promise?"

Jacob stood, still looking at the ground around his boots. Then he looked up and deep into Jasper Logan's eyes. "Yes sir," he said softly. "I will be there in the morning."

"Good," Jasper Logan said. "Tell your father he has my regards." And then he turned and walked steadily away.

Jacob could only stand and wonder if he had made the right decision. He could not tell for certain if he could trust the man or his words any longer. For as much as his words had made sense in a way, they were lacking something as well. Jacob stood and watched as Mr. Logan walked out of the family's lot. He watched him as he walked down the long sloping hill and skipped across the rocks to keep his boot dry. He watched him until he wound northward along the trail and disappeared behind the trees that lined the path as it entered Chariton proper.

Jacob studied his words again and again and wondered after them. He studied the man's gait as he walked to try and glean *something* from it. There was nothing he could get from it though, and in the end, nothing could quell his concerns about the man he called his employer. In the end, he would never look at Jasper Logan quite the same, ever again.

Chapter 15   Caught In The Moment

Evelyn Bates had been tending to her morning stitching when she had heard the church bells tolling. There was something about them that morning that made her uneasy and she went down earlier than normal to breakfast with Mrs. Harris. The two had made it a habit in recent weeks to eat together late in the morning, long after the other guests had eaten and gone.

"Good heavens," Mrs. Harris commented as Evelyn entered the room, "you look a fright this morning. Is something ailing you child?"

"What news have you of the bells ringing this morning?" Evelyn replied, ignoring her query.

"I've heard nothing of it dear," Mrs. Harris smiled reassuringly. "You needn't fret child. Had they been for any of our people, they'd have come to let us know of it by now. Perhaps we should go for a walk to the square to find out?"

Evelyn stood in a daze for a moment. She remembered when she could hear the bells from town carry upon the wind on the day that her husband had passed. On a day without much weather about and a gentle wind, you could hear the bells ringing for miles outside of town. She wondered if you could not hear them all the way in Albia if the wind were just so.

Just then the opening of the front door caused a draft to sweep through the old house and the pages of Mrs. Harris' recipe book flittered wildly. Mr. Gantry, a salesman of some sort who'd come to town to call upon local merchants, walked past the kitchen door on his way to his room. He stopped momentarily to tip his hat and exchange greetings.

"Morning ladies," he said politely. "I've just forgot some things in my room, Mrs. Harris. I shall go and retrieve them."

"Ah, very well Mr. Gantry," Mrs. Harris replied. "Oh, by the way, Mr. Gantry..."

The middle age man in the fancy suit stopped and spun around on his patent leather shoes to face them once again. He produced a feigned smile.

"Yes Ma'am?" he said politely and yet clearly impatiently.

"Have you any news regarding the bells this morning, Sir?" Mrs. Harris inquired.

"Ah, yes, the bells," he replied thoughtfully. "I believe that Mr. Hixson said there was some sort of accident at the creamery this morning. Some poor soul had been crushed and killed by a milk container of some sort. Must have been quite a milk container to do that, I should think."

"Thank you, Mr. Gantry," Mrs. Harris replied.

"You're quite welcome, Mrs. Harris," he replied as he spun back about to retrieve his things and complete whatever sale he was closing that morning.

"Now Evelyn," the older woman said, turning her attention back to the woman that had become as a daughter to her, "you needn't worry yourself. I'm certain that..."

Even before she had completed her sentence, Evelyn had darted from the room. Mrs. Harris had only turned to her in time to see the trailing of her dress as it swooped around the doorway behind her. Mrs. Harris might have been more alarmed but she knew from experience that someone would have stopped by then had it been Jasper Logan who was killed that day. She only turned and began to flip back through the pages of her cookbook and find the recipe that she had been studying before Evelyn had come down.

It was not considered appropriate for a woman to run then. Indeed, only when she feared that injury had occurred to young Ellis, had Evelyn ever done so since she was a child. And yet, here she was, running the walks in the finest part of town, the four blocks that separated Mrs. Harris' home from Logan's Creamery. She had still not righted her mind on whether or not to accept Jasper Logan's proposal, but she could not stand for it to end like this. The thought of losing him so soon after losing her husband was simply more than she could bear.

As she ran as best she could in her heeled boots, she thought of being alone in the world once again. Not alone, alone, for she would always have Ellis and her family, but alone without the comfort of a mate. It is a different sort of alone altogether and one that she did not care to experience. She had always known that she was beautiful and could find another man, and yet just then, she felt tiny and helpless and vulnerable and afraid at the thought of losing Jasper. Such was her state when she arrived at the doors of the creamery and queried the first man that stepped out of the door to light his pipe.

"What has happened here?" she demanded, having already cast all presumption of propriety into an irretrievable chasm by running all the way in front of God and everyone.

"Mr. Bell has been crushed," the man replied, raising an eyebrow to gauge her response to the news as he lit his pipe. She seemed to be relieved somewhat, and so, he too was relieved that she was not some ailing sister who he might have to comfort in the moment.

"Where is Mr. Logan?" she inquired further.

"He is gone on errands it would seem," the man replied, inhaling deeply through his pipe stem to bellow the burning embers of tobacco.

Evelyn should have been completely relieved as she turned about and headed back toward Mrs. Harris' house. The news should have been of comfort to her. As it was though, she had lost him in her mind already and she would not feel any comfort from any news until she had set eyes upon him once more. It was only as she walked the steps to Mrs. Harris' front door that she thought of how she must have appeared to the man at the creamery. She had not even thanked him before she had marched off. How rude she had behaved. It was certainly not in her character to behave in such a way as she had done. Could it be that she was really in *love* with Jasper Logan that she had acted in such a way? Or was it only her feelings of loss for her own departed husband that caused so much turmoil inside of her?

That day, Evelyn and Mrs. Harris would talk little of things. The older woman could tell when it was time for prying and talking and confessions, and when Evelyn simply required a stable, warm, quiet presence in her midst whilst she sorted things out inside of her own head. That day had been one of those days for certain, and Mrs. Harris spoke only of simple pleasantries while they strolled along the Chariton square and shopped.

All throughout the day, Evelyn scanned the crowds for him. Every hat had the possibility of being Jasper Logan until the head inside of it turned to reveal that it wasn't him. She thought of only him that day and what it would have done to her had she lost him that morning. Every head would turn and reveal that it was not him though, and she quietly suffered the heart wrenching agony of her irrational and unfounded fears.

As the day gave way to evening, she helped Mrs. Harris with dinner as had become her habit in recent weeks. Mrs. Harris insisted that she needn't do it, but really it was a pleasure of Evelyn's. It was as if she was a girl again, helping her own mother at home. Working in the kitchen with the elder woman was quite comforting.

For his own part, young Ellis would sit quietly at the small table inside the kitchen and play with his toys. Evelyn had used to worry that the boy seemed to require no company to be content, but lately it had seemed more of a blessing. The quiet sound effects he made while he played with toy soldiers had helped to assuage her through many of the troubling times she'd gone through after losing her husband. That day was no exception.

After dinner had been cleaned up and the guests retired to their rooms, Evelyn had read to Ellis in his bed until he fell fast asleep. She then wandered back downstairs and paced in the kitchen until Mrs. Harris invited her out on to the porch.

"Won't it be frightfully cold out there this evening?" Evelyn asked.

"Nonsense," Mrs. Harris replied. "We shall fire the porch stove dear, and the cool night air will do your chest good."

"Very well," Evelyn replied, and the two women headed outside onto the porch that lined the vast home.

Outside, on a far corner of the porch there was an extra parlor stove that had been placed for just such evenings by the deceased Mr. Harris. It was there beside that stove in the corner, that he would sit in his rocker in the evenings and smoke his pipe. Mrs. Harris had seldom fired it after he had passed, but she had continued to keep the wood box well stocked in case any of the guests desired to use it.

Mrs. Harris lit the tinder and slowly added sticks while she spoke of the people they had seen that day and all of the outdoor chores that spring brought with it for such a large yard and home. Evelyn only nodded and smiled politely, but both of them knew that her thoughts were elsewhere and any conversation on Mrs. Harris' part could only serve as background noise for what was at the forefront of her mind; Jasper Logan.

As the flames licked the top of the open stove door, Mrs. Harris set in a larger chunk of log on top and closed the door tight. The stove would not heat the outdoors, but it served the purpose of keeping the body warm on a cool night while the lungs breathed in the crisp, cold air. Just as Mrs. Harris thought of sharing how much she enjoyed it and how she would have to spend more evenings beside the stove, she turned to the footsteps approaching up the walk.

From out of the darkness, Jasper Logan stepped into the light of the porch and tipped his hat with a warm smile.

"Good evening ladies," he said. "Mrs. Harris. How are you?"

"Oh," Evelyn released a breath that she must have been holding all day. It was not a word so much as it was a sound that escaped her as she did so. She felt her knees weaken and she began to tremble as Jasper stepped forward and grasped her arm.

"Oh heavens," Mrs. Harris said slyly, "I've forgotten to remove something from the stove inside. Will you excuse me, please?"

"Of course," Logan said smiling.

"Thank you," the old woman said as she slipped inside the house, securing the door behind her so that neither of them would need worry about prying ears.

As she disappeared and the door was soundly shut, Evelyn threw herself into Jaspers arms and cried. "Oh Jasper," she said, "I thought I had lost you today. I thought..."

"Shhhh. There love. I am still with you," he replied, holding her closer to him than ever before and rubbing the back of her hair with his hand to comfort her. "All will be well," he said.

"I couldn't ever stand the thought of losing you," she whispered.

"And you never will, my love," he replied in a soft and comforting tone.

Remaining in his arms, she pushed herself away from him only enough to gaze into his eyes and touch his face. She had so missed being able to simply touch her husband's face since he had passed. She had dreamt of it a hundred times even.

"I'm sorry, Jasper," Evelyn said. "I feel so foolish. You must have had a horrible time of it today and here I am weeping like a school girl." Evelyn's face flushed with embarrassment.

"No, Evelyn. Don't apologize," he said. "It was an awful day indeed. Mr. Bell was a good man and it was a tragedy what happened. I only wished that there was some way that I could have taken his place. There was no way that I could have known. It was a terrible accident. And yet, I can't help but feel that it was somehow my fault; my responsibility. I..."

Jasper Logan pushed her away slightly and turned his head away from Evelyn so that she couldn't see his face. A better actor perhaps could have produced a real tear or two, but they were not in him. He could only look away solemnly and feign to be hiding something that did not exist.

It worked marvelously though, and Evelyn held fast to his arm weeping. "It was God's will," she said. "You could not have known, Jasper. And I am so grateful that nothing happened to you. I would not have been able to live with myself. I love you so."

"Then marry me," Jasper replied. With the words, he dropped to his knee and looked up at her. We have danced around the issue long enough Evelyn. You say that you cannot live without me, and yet you insist on putting me off and keeping me as if a toy upon some cruel string. Marry me," he pronounced once again.

"Oh Jasper..." she said, looking down into his eyes. With her hand she wiped his dark wavy hair from in front of his eyes. "I..."

"Providence has brought us together Evelyn, and divine intervention saved me from peril today. There is a reason for it. I am certain of it. And that reason is you Evelyn. That reason is us. We were meant to be love. Marry me," he finished.

Evelyn looked into his eyes and struggled to gain composure of her heart with her mind. Her heart had taken hold of her emotions and had led her through the entire day though, and all of the reservations that were in her brain could not affect her course of action. "Yes, Jasper," she said softly, caressing his cheek even as the turmoil inside her made her feel queasy. "I will marry you," she finished.

Without much further for either of them to say, Jasper rose to his feet once more. The two held each other there on the front porch of Mrs. Harris' Inn beside a warm glowing woodstove for most of the evening. The clear night sky and the stars that had shone upon them gave way to the ominous foreboding of thunder clouds and flashes of lightning lit up the Chariton sky. Somewhere off in the distance, a terrible storm was brewing.

Chapter 16   Hiram's Treasure

As spring of 1870 gave way to early summer, Hiram Wilson could barely contain his elation. It was already June. For as much as each day seemed to last an eternity and it seemed that he would never see *her* again, each day brought him closer to the moment when he would be reunited with Clara and she would finally be his. Each morning then, he sprang awake, marking the passing of yet another day and drawing closer the time when they would finally be together. His heart beat solidly in his chest those mornings, his breath drew in the moist morning air with vigor, and he raced to greet the day, as if his vigor and enthusiasm would cause time itself to pass by more rapidly.

In preparation for the day, he had stolen away with his one valuable possession in this world. It was the only thing that he truly owned that was his aside from the trinkets and letters that he kept squirreled away inside the wall of the wood shed. He had taken the saddle that his grandfather had given him years before and sold it to Mr. Damm. With that and the portion of his wage that he withheld from his father, Hiram had amassed a fortune of nearly sixty dollars. It wasn't nearly enough, but to Hiram it was a fortune and far more cash money than he had ever seen before.

Hiram had worked another full day, from before the sun had risen until it had set, and spent each moment of it dreaming of Clara. He wondered if her hair was still long and wavy and dark as it had been before. He guessed which flower her perfume most resembled; which of her letters she most smelled like. He thought about her eyes, blue like the heavens above or a spring fed lake. They were pools that you could gaze deep inside of and let your soul swim about within.

It had been but less than two years since last he had seen her when they had gone back to visit his aunt in Illinois. It was then that he had looked into those beautiful eyes of hers and had stolen a kiss. Rather, he had been mesmerized within those eyes at the moment, and she had stolen the kiss. But either way, it was the most amazing moment of his life. It was the memory of that moment, of the tenderness of her kiss, of the beauty of her eyes and the heavenly scent of her hair that carried him through each day, each abuse from his father, and every hardship in his young life. All of it would be as a far away bad dream that had happened to someone else when they were finally together once more.

Today, he had only the scented letters and the memories of her, but soon he would have so much more. Soon, she would be in his arms with her head rested upon his shoulder. Soon they would hold one another in a place called Iowa and together, they would carve out a life. There would be bountiful harvests and a table filled with food and children. He'd dreamed it so as if it had already happened. He believed in that dream as if it had been a premonition from God Himself of things to come.

Hiram stowed away about half of the money that Mr. Damm had paid him that week. As the hour of their wedding approached, he withheld more and more of his meager pay from his father. Each time he would say that Mr. Damm was shorter and shorter of cash and had promised to settle the difference at some future date. Lying, it seemed, had become all too easy for him those days, and lying to his father was the easiest lie of them all. Besides, by the time that future date came due, he would be long gone. His father would be left to wonder where he had gone to. The old man would probably even pay a visit to Mr. Damm to retrieve his son's owed wages, but by then Hiram and Clara would be far away from there, together and happy.

Hiram placed the plank carefully back into its rightful spot upon the wood shed wall. More and more of the mortar caulking had crumbled and fallen to the floor each day, but by then he no longer bothered keeping up with it. There was little reason that time of year for his father to be in the wood shed at all, and soon, every treasure that the plank concealed would be gone when he left to meet Clara.

As added insurance, Hiram gathered up an armload of wood for the cook stove and carried it into the cabin. Outside, the last faint orange hues in the Western skies were yielding slowly to the darkness of night. His father was nowhere to be found.

Hiram had no sooner started the old cook stove and filled the cabin with the light of lanterns than he heard the horses and wagon rumbling to a stop outside. Even through the thick hewn oak walls of the old cabin, he could hear his father outside cursing at the animals as he unhitched them. Hiram hurried to set a pot upon the stove and begin mixing some flour for biscuits. If he appeared to be busy enough in the throes of his work making supper, there was a chance the old man might pay little mind of him.

"God damn you, you...," Elias broke off his sentence and only incoherent drunken babbling could be heard through the walls as he staggered toward the door.

"Good evening Father," Hiram said pleasantly as the door opened and the old man staggered inside. Hiram tried not to look at him, and instead focused intently upon mixing and moving pots about and such.

Elias spun about in his boots to face his son. As he did so, the door slammed behind him from the wind and he fell backwards until he came to a standing rest with his buttocks pressed into the wall of the cabin.

"Where in the hell have you been?" Elias said angrily.

"I have only just returned from Mr. Damm's, Papa," he replied as he turned to face him.

It was going to be a bad night. Hiram could see by the blackness of his father's eyes that he was on a mean drunk. As old Elias drank, his eyes grew red with bloodshot, and then glossed over into a sparkly, dull sheen. But when he was on a bad drunk on strong whiskey or homebrew, his eyes would turn completely black as the pupils seemed to enlarge to match the extent of his rage.

"Where is my money?" Elias spoke as he pushed himself off of the wall and staggered forward.

"I gave it all to you before Pa," Hiram said. "Mr. Damm said he will pay me the rest in two weeks."

"What say you?" Elias replied.

By now Elias was standing beside him, bobbing to and fro, back and forth. The stench of whiskey oozed into Hiram's nostrils. It was thick and moist and caused his stomach to turn over as he inhaled. Over the years, Hiram had come to equate that smell with a good many things, all of them bad. It was the reason that he himself never took a drink. But most of all, just then, it just made him ill to his stomach.

"I said Mr. Damm said that he will..." Hiram began to reply.

"Liar!" Elias screamed, spitting thick whiskey scented mucus on Hiram's face as he yelled.

Elias reached upon the stove, swiping up the skillet and struck Hiram across the side of the head with it. As he swung it, the scalding hot lard splattered them both before Elias stumbled backwards onto the floor. Even before his body came to a full rest, Elias grabbed his face and neck and screamed in agony. "You son of a bitch!" he yelled. "I should kill you for this!"

Hiram grabbed at his right ear and cleared out the burning grease as best he could. Some had splattered on his cheek and even as he rubbed it, he could feel the skin beginning to boil. Most of it was in his hair and along the back of his neck though. As he rose from the edge of the table where he had had fallen from the blow of the skillet, he looked down at his father who was writhing on the floor and cursing between screams.

At first, he thought he should help him up but the thought was quickly dismissed as he felt the piercing burning inside of his ear. It was then, for the first time in his life that the thought passed through his head of raising the skillet high above him and striking his own father dead. It was a sin to think of such things, sure enough, but there it was burning through Hiram like the sizzling grease within his ear and on his cheek and neck.

Hiram pushed the thought from his mind and walked around his father who could only lay there holding his face and moaning in agony between curses. He could not bring himself to kill him. And he could not strike him even once for fear that he would be unable to stop if ever he set about starting it.

"Come and help me!" his father demanded, seeing Hiram headed for the door. "Damnit, boy, you come here and help me!"

Hiram stopped for only a second and turned about and looked at his father. The aging drunk lay there up the floor, the skin on his face bubbling with festering red burns. It would all be over soon enough, he thought to himself and he turned to walk out the door and lock himself safely in the wood shed. He'd be hungry again sure enough, but he could be with Clara for a spell and smell her letters and read her words, and all of the pain and worry could be left behind while Hiram dreamed of her.

As he turned his back once more, and right before the door closed behind him, he heard these words; "Go on then you coward. Go on and get! I wish you'd never been born! I wish you'd died that night instead of your mother, you God damned coward!"

As the door of the cabin closed behind him, Hiram heard the words echo inside of him. They passed through his burning ear and traveled directly to his heart which grew heavier until it was as a weight that he could hardly stand inside of him. In the few steps between the cabin and the wood shed, Hiram found himself immobilized by the words and they left a stinging in him far worse than the burning oil had.

Sapped of all of his strength and every ounce of will inside of him, Hiram fell to his knees upon the ground and began to sob uncontrollably. He wept as mightily as he had ever wept, even as a child. He wept for the loss of his mother and even the loss of his father. He wept for the nights that he had spent as a child in bed with no supper, and he wept for the cold and hungry nights he had spent in the woodshed. A sadness filled every corner of his being with a dark foreboding like he had never before known and all he could do was sob and cry and weep and ask "why?"

Hiram did not even have a singular question to attach to the 'why.' He could only feel the heaviness of his heart, the sickness in his stomach, and the emptiness inside of him unlike anything he had ever experienced before. As he knelt there in the dirt weeping, Hiram knew that this was how his life was meant to be. He knew that nothing good would ever come of him. He even scolded himself for ever believing that someone like Clara would really love him, or that someone like her *could* ever really love him. His father had been right all along, he thought to himself. He was as worthless as they came and as stupid as a blind ass. He too, at that moment, wished that he had never been born and not even the thoughts of Clara would clear his head of the darkness that reigned over him. All that night, Hiram wept.

Chapter 17   Clara

Clara Smith sat at her writing desk and took out a colored parchment. The stationary had been a Christmas gift from a well to do uncle back east whose trade it was to deal in such fine things. It had been meant, she was told, to use to write to him more often. He had joked that since his own sister would not write him often that he would have to rely upon young Clara to keep him abreast of the goings on within their family. Mostly though, she had reserved the prettiest of it to write to Hiram.

She set a piece of flush pink paper in front of her and gently dipped her pen into the ink well.

June 10 , 1870

My Dearest Hiram ,

I Pray This Letter Reaches You Well. I Have Not Heard From You In Some Time And I Fear That Mother Has Stolen Your Letters Or Worse, That You Have Finally Tired Of Me. I Have News That We Shall Be Departing For Illinois Sooner Than Expected. Indeed, Papa Has Announced That We Are Leaving Very Soon.
It Would Seem That There Shall Be Two Weddings In The Near Future As My Sister Is Set To Remarry. We Expect To Stay On In Her Company Until After She Has Married In The City Of Chariton, Iowa. We Shall Arrive There On The Third Day Of July. I Pray That You Shall Come For Me There. You Are My Love, My Life, My All.

Yours In Eternal Love,

Clara Mary Smith

Clara set down her quill pen and carefully capped the ink bottle. Then, reaching to the small stand beside her desk she selected a tiny bottle of lavender perfume and squeezed two little puffs of fragrance on to the parchment. It seemed a quaint thing to do to her, even if it had probably all been worn well into the air before it ever reached him. But like her squiggly capital letters, she felt that it proved at least to herself, how much she loved Hiram by the level of care she put into each letter.

Folding the parchment and then lightly licking the crease, she pressed it firmly with the edges of her thumbs until it lay flat in squarely folded perfection. Then she placed it inside of a matching envelope and addressed it. She would drop it by the post master's office the next morning when she went for her walk. Clara placed the letter under a book and closed her writing desk.

She wondered what Hiram was doing just then. She could scarcely wait until the moment that he would ride into Chariton to steal her away. She imagined herself walking along the street with her sister and her parents when out from a cloud of dust would emerge Hiram upon a thick necked chestnut stallion. She had no idea how the horse had become a stallion, let alone a chestnut stallion, but such was her fantasy and she had learned not to question her fantasies. Life was disappointing enough without going out of your way to borrow troubles for your own self.

He would ride right up to them and make some bold proclamation to her parents as he grabbed her and pulled her up behind him on the horse. Then they would ride off together into some magical adventure where they would always be together, always happy, always in love. She knew little about love herself, but she knew without question that Hiram loved her. And that meant more than all else. He was not terribly tall or terribly handsome, but he was sweet beyond measure and most of all, he loved her. He loved her fully and completely and cared for her more deeply than she could imagine another human being caring for her. It was *his* love, more than anything that caused her to love him so. Any girl could marry. But only a select few would be fortunate enough to find a man who worshipped them and adored them as if they were a Greek Goddess, and such was the love that Hiram expressed for her.

Clara exhaled and swooned at the thought of him and the way he looked at her. She was starry eyed and dreaming still when her mother called her down for dinner. "Soon my love," she said softly. "Very soon," and Clara drew a deep breath, fixed her dress and walked out of the room. Every movement she made was for the day to come, when she would finally be his, and their life together could begin in earnest. What wonder that it is to be loved thus, she thought and she smiled at the dreams of what all was to come. Soon. Very soon.

Chapter 18   Return To Safety

Sheriff Gaylord Lyman awoke to find Sol already waiting up for him. He started his morning coffee the same as he had a thousand mornings before that one. As he did so, he heard the shuffle of Jacob's tired dragging feet as he walked into the kitchen. He knew they'd be there that morning waiting for him to finish the story. He'd promised it to Sol the evening before when he'd rode in late. He told him that there'd be other days, that he was retiring and soon he'd be on the farm with them most all of the time. He had tried to convince him to let it go until then, but Sol had insisted that they had waited long enough. Reluctantly, Gaylord had relented to the desires of his son. He owed it to them, he figured.

Turning about, he looked into Jacob's eyes. They were swollen and puffy and lacked the bright clarity of a young man well rested. Since the accident at the creamery, Jacob had come to have some ghosts of his own keeping him awake at night. The Sheriff looked at him sympathetically. He knew that Jacob had lost more than a friend that day. Ever since then, he didn't have the same ambition or desire to advance at

128

the creamery that he once had. Gaylord knew full well that in time, his son would leave the creamery behind him, even if the boy had not yet reached the same conclusion.

Taking his seat at the head of the table, Gaylord turned to Sol as he sipped his coffee. Sol was as wide eyed as he'd ever seen him so early. He had the look that Jacob once had adorned before he set off to work in the mornings.

"Well," he inquired of Sol. "Where was I?"

The Injuns was following you, but not coming in close to kill you Pa," Sol replied.

"Oh yes," Gaylord responded, taking one last sip off his steaming cup of coffee before he continued, "thank you, son."

 Sheriff Gaylord Lyman gazed into the coffee once again and took his mind back to that day out on the prairie. With a steely gaze into the darkness of the cup, he continued,

"It was brutally hot during the day and bitterly cold at night. Like I said, the temperature must swing fifty degrees or more in the course of a single day and night out there. The beautiful huge sky that I had so admired and adored only a few days prior became like a nightmare that never seemed to end. I could set my sights upon a small grove of trees or the like as of a morning and walk all day and not reach it before nightfall. It just went on forever. And always, they were there, following within plain sight of me when I looked back.

It was so hot and dry out there. My body was done for. I knew that they could have come riding in and kill me at any second, any time they wanted to, and I thought about just sitting down and letting them do it. Making them end the ordeal instead of watching me die slowly in their own sick damned version of cat and mouse.

By the third evening I was barely moving at all. I hadn't eaten anything and worst of all, I hadn't had so much as a drop of water. Even more than that though, even worse than the thirst and the hunger and the Indians, was the sadness of guilt of what had happened back there. I couldn't help thinking that if only I hadn't drank that night that it might have ended differently. I might have been able to stop them. And why was I spared? Was it because I was the only one too drunk to rouse, so they thought it would be funny to let me be? Was it because I, and I alone, had not been wearing a uniform? What? Why had they left me to bare witness?

Looking back, I believe the latter to be the truth of the thing. I believe that they wanted to send a message to the rest of the country about what would happen to any more soldiers who ventured any further into their country. And, looking back now, I think they might have followed me all that way and pushed me on, staying behind me like that, just to make damned certain that I made it.

Anyways, I was just about done for when I lit over a small hilltop and there before me was a lush, green valley. It was a branch of the Loup River. The Middle Loup I believe. We hadn't followed it before as we had veered off South of it as we rode out. But there it was. So I had not only staggered for three days, but I had done so off course to the north. It turned out though that my lack of direction saved my life that day.

It was the dry season and where I first came upon the thing there was no water running or even standing, but I was able to dig a shallow hole in the sand and strike water. It was warm and foul tasting, but it might have been the coldest, clearest spring water on that day the way I took to it. I mean, I must have just sat and drank for the better part of an hour and wet my head and face in the stuff. I even tried to dig a bigger hole and submerge my whole damned body in it.

I knew the course of the river would lead me just north of La Grande Island. Then I could head south when it veered off to the east, so I followed it. As it turned out, after an hour or so on the fourth morning, I hadn't needed to try and dig that hole after all because I hit a trickle of standing water, then a small running creek. By the end of the day, it was a river true enough. I was even able to pick up little odds and ends to put on my belly too.

We had ridden slowly out across the plains of Nebraska Territory for three and a half days. I had no idea how long it would take a man to walk the eighty or so miles we had traveled. But I knew it when I arrived. The answer is six days and five nights straight because that is how long it took me to do it.

When the La Grande Island settlement came into view I turned to look back at the Indians who had followed me all that way. I was hoping that they would keep on following me all the way in, so the Germans of La Grande Island could man their rifles and lay them low. It was as if they read my mind at the very thought though, because as I stopped and looked at them, they casually turned their horses with ours still in tow, and rode away into the setting sun of the Nebraska Prairie.

Six days of misery and guilt. Six days of thirst and hunger. Six days with the strong stench of death upon me as I had been covered in the blood of my mules and my cohorts. Six days and I staggered into the La Grande Island settlement nearly dead. Six days.

That evening, one of the settlers took me into their home where I was told later, that I slept for the next two nights in a row after eating a small meal of sausages and a biscuit. When I did finally wake up, I awoke to the smell of fresh blood on the prairie and slaughtered men, and Indians who followed me into my dreams.

Most nights, they're still there. The Indians are still following me. My fellow traveler's bodies... I dream horrible, unspeakable dreams some nights boys," he finished, tears welling up in the corners of his eyes.

As if on cue by some invisible stage director, Bella shuffled into the kitchen and smiled a warm morning greeting at her sons. She was so proud of them, each one for different reasons, but most of all, she was proud that they were all three there and Jacob and Sol were almost grown men. All throughout the 1860's Bella had watched friends and family alike lose children and husbands to one sickness or the next, but here she was, uniquely blessed among the mothers of the day to still have each of her spawn and first husband all in tact and accounted for.

"Good morning, Ma!" The Sheriff said, rising to greet her. He kissed her softly upon her cheek.

Gaylord had always done that sort of thing. He had never been of the ilk that most men seemed to adhere to. He was always kissing her on her cheek, or holding her hand while they walked. During the winter months, he could even be seen holding her close and squeezing her small body tightly into his side. Some women of the town thought it to be scandalous for a Christian couple to carry on that way in public, but most of them were only jealous and lacking husbands who showed them similar affection any time, day or night, public or otherwise.

"Good morning, Pa," she said, smiling softly back at him and kissing the cheek as she filled her nostrils with the scents of strong coffee that wafted from his person. How she had come to love that smell upon him in the mornings. It was his trademark. She had never learned to enjoy the tar that her husband called coffee in the mornings, but she always had loved the smell of him from it.

What mischief are the three of you boys up to on this fine morning?" she inquired, sensing *something* a bit queer about the expression on Sol's face.

"Nothin' at all Ma," Gaylord replied. "Me and the boys was just swapping old war stories is all."

"I see," she said. "Well, before you boys scoot out for the day, do you reckon it might be possible for you to tend to the handle on the well pump. It has been giving me fits for sometime and war stories of my own to tell. Yesterday I fear that it finally broke altogether."

"Of course, ma," Gaylord replied. "I'll tend to it first thing."

"Thank you," she said.

"And while I have you all here," the sheriff announced, "there is something that I want to tell you."

"What is it, Pa?" Sol inquired, looking up for the first time from his own cup of coffee where he had been staring intently, trying to clear his face of whatever tell his mother had taken notice of.

"Well," Gaylord replied. "I have decided that there are too many well pump handles on this farm that need tended to, and too many Ma's and boys who require my services more than the people of Lucas County. What I'm trying to say is that this will be my last term as sheriff. This fall, when election comes about, I'm not going to run. It's time for me to come home."

"Oh Gaylord," Bella cried, and she ran into his arms and instantly began to weep. She had never said a single word about it. She had never complained about the long hours, or doing his chores on the farm, or raising his sons. And she had certainly never let on how scared she had been every single time that he had walked out that front door wearing a badge. The dangers of such a position were numerous she knew, especially throughout the war years along the Missouri border, but she had never said a single, solitary word to him about any of it. But now that she heard him say it, she was overwhelmed by her relief. All she could do was cry and hold him close.

Chapter 19 Lucas County Courthouse

Sheriff Gaylord Lyman walked as he had done a thousand times before into town. This day was special though because he and Jacob walked together. As the elder Lyman walked past the flat, still shimmering water of the city lake, he felt that the day marked a new beginning; a new chapter in his life. Jacob talked of the creamery, and Mr. Logan, and how he had not gotten over the incident that had killed Mr. Bell.

"I just don't know how much longer I can work for a man I have no respect for, Pa," he'd confided that day.

It was as if in the sharing of the story of the Nebraska Territory that he had formed a new bond with his older two sons. Gaylord rejoiced inside at the thought of it and spoke to his son in kind, as one man might speak to another, instead of a father to a growing son.

"A man has got to sew his own fields son, for he and he alone will reap what he harvests," the sheriff replied. "You've got a good heart inside of you, Jacob, and a good head upon your shoulders. Think well on things, but trust in your judgments and do what is right for you and you will grow old with few regrets," he said thoughtfully.

"I will do just that. I can't stand the thought of working for a man I don't respect for twenty or thirty years," Jacob said.

"Life is all about choices and every man has to follow their own road Jacob. No matter which one you choose, I am proud of the man you've become," Gaylord said as he held back a small tear that he felt forming in the corner of his wrinkled eye.

"Thanks Pa," Jacob replied and for only a moment the two stood looking into one another's eyes before Jacob turned and headed off for the creamery.

"Have a fine day, Son," Gaylord called after him. He stood for a few moments longer and watched as his son trotted off to work. Truly, he had become a man. Gaylord marveled to himself about how, through no fault of his own, his son had grown into such a remarkable individual.

Jacob had always had the look of his father about him, but on the inside he had the good heart and quick wit of his mother. Gaylord silently rejoiced throughout the rest of his walk to the courthouse that morning, for not only the grown son he'd just seen off to work, but for the knowledge that he would soon be retiring from the profession that had kept him away from all of them for far too long.

He could never really know for sure why he had been spared out there in the Nebraska Territory all those years before. There had been so many times that he reckoned that he should have died out there. Inside of him, he felt a guilt that he could not put into words for simply still being among the living. To the Indians, he had been but a messenger to tell others what would happen to soldiers who ventured too far into their territory. But to Gaylord Lyman, they were harbingers of death who served to remind him each day that he was not living his life to the fullest.

For as much he owed it to his sons and wife to be there for them, he felt deep within his soul that he was letting the men who died on the prairie down too. He had failed to live up to the promise that a survivor owed the dead. On this day, however, having announced his intentions to leave his work behind him in the fall and better get to know the fine young men that he called his sons, he felt an overwhelming joy in his soul. Finally, he would be going home to them. Just a few more months and his promise would finally be fulfilled.

The sheriff was still smiling to himself as he strolled across the courthouse lawn. The small two story brick structure was a comforting building to him. It had been constructed some twenty years before to replace the old log cabin that had originally served as the county hub. Although the current structure was much larger, it was also becoming increasingly too small for the growing county around it. Not only did it simply not have the room to house the growing number of records and clerks required to run a county, but it paled in comparison to the grand courthouses that were being constructed throughout the country.

But still, for all of its faults, the sheriff liked the building. It probably had a great deal to do with the fact that it was that building, more than any other, that had served as the beacon of relief after long rides out on the trail. He had ridden most of the night on many occasions and he was never really home from a journey until he reached the comfort and solitude of the Lucas County Courthouse.

Inside, he was greeted by the creaky hardwood floor and the smell of coffee on the small stove mingling in the air with fresh ink and aging documents. Deputy Clark sat with his boots planted upon their shared desk. Most nights, Roy would be found at his home a few blocks off the square, but they had a prisoner in their charge at the time, so he spent his shift there. It was hard at times for both men, being the only two paid lawmen in the entire county, but it was especially hard on Sheriff Lyman who felt his duty called upon him to be about whenever there was any business to tend to.

Deputy Clark swung his feet off the desk when Sheriff Lyman entered.

"Good morning, Roy," Gaylord said merrily.

"Good morning Sheriff," the deputy replied.

"How's our prisoner?" he inquired.

"Fine Sheriff," Israel replied, smiling from his chair in the corner behind the deputy.

Israel Hixson had taken to following in the footsteps of many other abolitionists before the war and refused to pay taxes in support of an unjust government. The difference was, however, that even throughout the war, and after the defeat of the confederate states and slavery, Israel held fast to his radical views and kept right on refusing to pay. Every once in a while a new writ would come through on him and the Sheriff would be forced to go out and arrest him until the district judge made it back to town.

Israel had become such a fixture at the jail that no one bothered to lock his cell any more, or even put him in it. The aging man was of no threat and even helped out by making coffee and keeping the stove going. More than anything, Deputy Clark stayed overnight while he was in their charge just to keep him company. The two could be found most nights playing checkers and exchanging stories at an hour when the rest of the county was fast asleep.

"You look to be in awful good spirits this morning," Deputy Clark raised an eyebrow in suspicion at the jaunty sheriff.

"I am," Gaylord replied.

"What ails you sheriff?" Israel interjected.

"Well sir," the sheriff replied, "I have announced to my family and now to you two esteemed gentlemen, my intentions come this fall to hand over the reigns of this here one horse operation, and retire from my post."

"What?" Deputy Clark sat up abruptly in his chair. The light mood of the morning suddenly changed as he began to consider the ramifications of the announcement.

"That's right Roy," Gaylord replied. "You're going to have to step up. It's time for you to do more than just play checkers all night to earn your wage."

"He doesn't even do that very well," Israel remarked with a chuckle. "I beat him ten games out of fifteen last night."

"Well, I'll be. You're really leaving me?" Deputy Clark looked at the Sheriff's eyes and studied them hard to make sure he wasn't joking with him again. It was not uncommon for their exchanges to include some sort of practical tomfoolery, especially in the mornings.

"Yes, sir," Gaylord looked him back in the eye so he knew that he was in earnest. "I am. It is due time that I tended to my own flock. I've done for the people of this county long enough. It is due time that I took to doing for my own before they're all grown and gone."

"Well, good for you, Sheriff," Israel said, as he rose from his chair. "Congratulations. This calls for a drink," he said as he poured the sheriff a cup of coffee and then topped of their own cups.

"To your flock," Israel announced as he raised his cup into the air.

"To the Sheriff," Deputy Clark followed, "may he change his mind and save me the grief of the position!"

Sheriff Lyman chuckled, and the three men all took a sip together. It was official. He had made it public. Soon, he would be a farmer; a civilian whose interests seldom would go beyond the fences that surrounded his property. His only charge in life would be the tending of his livestock, the nurturing of his crops, and the well being of his own wife and children. He drew a deep, satisfied breath, and as he exhaled, he could feel a deep sense of satisfaction within his breast.

Looking out the window, the town square began to slowly show signs of life. Doors were being opened and shop keeps were sweeping the walks in front of their businesses. Chariton had grown so much in the last decade. It was no longer a frontier town, but a real American town, full of the prosperity and opportunity that marked any good town of the time. Soon, it would be a city in its' own right.

Throughout his tenure as Sheriff of Lucas County, Gaylord Lyman had played an important role in the town and the county. He had made the streets safe and settled a hundred disputes over the years that would have otherwise ended in gunplay and death. Now, those days were coming to an end and so was his time as the sheriff. He was proud of what he had done, of his part in it all. But as he had told his own son that very morning, a man need only to think well upon things and trust in his judgment, then do what is right for him and he will grow old with few regrets.

Standing there, looking out at the town as it sprang to life, Gaylord Lyman knew that it was the right time and he was deeply satisfied with his decision. What's more, he knew that if he lived to be a hundred he would never live to regret having left to spend more time with his wife and children. Finally, he would be going home.

Chapter 20   Prior Engagement

The engagement of Evelyn Bates to Jasper Logan was the talk of the town those days. Jasper had made it a point to announce their intentions formally at the opera house within 48 hours of her acceptance. He had correctly sensed that she still had her reservations, but with the entire community involved he knew full well that a woman of Evelyn's social standing would not easily be able to reconsider.

In exchange for her coerced loyalty, Jasper had promised her a rare day of leave from his business affairs to take her for a ride in the Lucas County countryside. He had gone in early to the creamery to see to his affairs and had left Jacob Lyman in his charge to tend to the daily concerns of the creamery. Indeed, Jacob had become a trusted leader within the creamery. Even men as much as thirty years his elder would defer to his sound judgment on most matters. He was well upon his way to becoming the creamery superintendent. Being left in charge by Jasper was just one more step in the young man's ascent within the Logan Empire.

Jasper Logan, accustomed to the frugal living of a single male and not one prone to extravagance in his daily life, even marked the day with the purchase of new carriage. He had told her the evening before when they made the buggy's maiden voyage that he had required a more suitable form of transportation if he was to be seen with one of Chariton's most prominent wives. Evelyn, for her part, had been pleased by the gesture and the kind words, but remained through it all, deeply affected by the growing worry in the pit of her stomach that something was amiss between them.

Still, it was a beautiful early summer morning when Jasper arrived at Mrs. Harris' Inn to pick her up. He was dressed in his finest and smiling warmly as he entered the kitchen with a new derby hat in his hands. Somehow, even though he had just removed the hat, his dark wavy hair remained perfect.

"Good morning to you, Mr. Logan," Mrs. Harris spoke genuinely in fondness as she kneaded her bread dough for that evening.

"And to you, Mrs. Harris," he replied. "You are looking fine as ever, if I may be so bold as to say so," he continued. Charming women of every sort was his specialty, and his gift with it was not lost upon him.

"You may say so," the old woman replied smiling warmly and blushing slightly, "and what brings you here on this fine morning?" Mrs. Harris teased.

"I have come to claim my future bride, Ma'am," he said, smiling toward Evelyn with a wink, who sat at the table sipping her coffee.

"I was beginning to wonder when you might notice me," she said dryly, pretending to be offended.

"How could I help but notice you," Logan replied smartly, stepping toward her and raising her hand to kiss it. "But whatever is a gentleman to do when in the company of *both* of the county's most beautiful women?"

Jasper looked up into Evelyn's eyes and gave a quick wink, then raised an eyebrow toward Mrs. Harris. There came no reply from the old woman, but her face emitted a brighter shade of red as his words passed over her ears. Evelyn smiled at him and shook her head. He *was* a charming and handsome man, she had thought to herself, admiring his shining eyes and perfect hair. If there was anyone worthy of her affections it must be him.

A more perfect day for a ride could not have been imagined. While the sun shone brightly, a storm raged well off to the south and a cool wind blew across the shimmering leaves of the elms that lined the streets of the bustling town. If you had lived in Chariton for even a few years, you had witnessed a steady growth and the improvements that came with a rise in the population were beginning to become more noticeable.

For at least two blocks radiating out from the town square, gas lanterns had been recently installed. At night they cast a beautiful flickering light onto the otherwise dark and desolate streets. By day they were equally as beautiful to behold as the scrolls and designs within the molded cast iron, and shiny black painted surfaces glistened in the sun, imparting a bit of big city elegance upon the town.

There was even talk of paving the city streets on and around the town square and even constructing a new courthouse. The two story brick structure was not nearly old enough to replace yet, but it was not nearly large enough to suit the needs of the county or the egos of its leading citizens. Besides, the design of the thing was causing it to begin to fail even as the mortar still hardened. Some even talked of using the bricks from the existing courthouse to pave the first roads around it.

Jasper stood, and holding her hand, lifted Evelyn into the carriage. It really was a divine carriage. It had plush velvet seats and fancy brass lanterns and shiny brass detailing all over it. The black paint shimmered in the slightest hint of light and even had reflected the starlight the evening before during their first short ride.

Pulling them were a pair of the most majestic black and white paints that Evelyn had ever seen. They were from Jasper's private stock, of course, but still she had never seen the pair before. They were huge, magnificent animals for paints, as if they had been bred with a draft horse somewhere in their bloodlines, but retained the maneuverability of much smaller animals.

Climbing aboard, Jasper grasped the reigns and with a quick snap of them, they were off. Evelyn did so enjoy a good ride and it was truly the perfect day for one. She could not tell if it was due to the plush cushioned seats or the fancy springs of the buggy, but it was the smoothest, most delightful ride she could ever recollect. Truly, if *this* was indicative of what life with Jasper Logan was going to be like for her, she might well become accustomed to it, to him, and to her doubts. After all, what little girl did not desire to grow and one day to become a princess, or at the very least, be treated like one?

Passing through the city streets, it seemed that everyone in town was about that morning. More than that, it seemed that every citizen of the county would momentarily cease their activity to watch them pass. To Evelyn it was as if they were the royal couple of the town and all eyes were admiring them. It could have only been the beautiful horses that drew the stares, or the shiny new buggy, by far the fanciest in the county now. Still, it seemed to her that it was the handsomeness of passengers that drew their eyes upon them. What woman did not desire to be riding in her place? What man did not desire to be in his?

One woman dropped her eggs as she emerged from her chicken house and looked up to see them pass. Another, a man, ceased the hoeing of his garden and leaned upon his implement to watch them as they rode by. They were the envy of every body in Chariton and to Evelyn it was marvelous.

Even more marvelous than being the belle of the town however, were the incredible views in the countryside. Lucas County was one of slow rolling hills and tree filled shallow valleys, each one with its own creek flowing through it, like the Whitebreast or Cedar or the Chariton River itself.

They stopped for a picnic upon a small knob overlooking the latter. Beneath them the banks of the Chariton River could be seen flowing gently past. Above them the Sky provided an amazing scene of far off thunder clouds with flashes of lightening views through the foliage of gigantic cottonwood trees whose leaves shimmered gently in the cool breezes and gusts. It seemed to Evelyn as if the cottonwoods along the banks of the Chariton must have been among the oldest living things in the world. They were so immense, so grand, that it was as if God Himself has planted them with his own hand only moments after molding the earth itself.

Spreading a blanket upon the ground, Jasper produced a basket with cheeses and buttermilk and crackers and butter. Evelyn loved Jasper's buttermilk most of all. His creamery was known for its cheese foremost, but to her it was the thick frothy buttermilk that she most enjoyed.

"I love your buttermilk," she said to him as she sipped from the jar.

146

"I love you," he replied, smiling at her and looking deep into her eyes in hopes that he would see a reflection of his affections.

Still, it was not there as he had hoped. She remained distant somehow. It was beyond his understanding how after doing everything correct, everything perfectly, that she failed to return his affection in the same way he felt for her. She had agreed to marry him, but still there was a distance in her eyes that he could only assume had something to do with her deceased husband. It will come with time, he reassured himself.

"It is such a perfectly beautiful day," she said, shifting the subject to cut the odd tension that hung in the air between them just then. "We should go to the show this evening at the opera house. I am told they are a wonderful lot of performers there at the moment. Some group out of Chicago I think," she said, taking another sip from her jar.

"I cannot do it this evening, love," he replied. "I am to attend a meeting of The Anti Horse Thief Society tonight."

"What a silly thing that is, Jasper. A secretive men's club full of secretive men no doubt. I would think that the desires of your fiancé might trump such a meeting," Evelyn said, looking thoughtfully at the clouds as they rolled past above them.

"I have been elected to head the chapter for the year darling," he replied. "The people of the community reply upon me to be at the meeting."

"I haven't heard of any horse thefts as of late anyhow, have you?" she said.

"Not as of late," he replied, "but the men who fear such things have elected me as the chair. What's more, those same men

147

all supply their families with goods from my creamery and I can ill afford to let them down based upon a whim."

"It must be so very drab to have such great responsibilities resting upon your shoulders all of the time," she quipped.

"It is," Logan replied irritably, having correctly sensed the intentions of her remark. "But it is an engagement that I had prior to our own engagement, and I have every intention of keeping it. We shall go to the show another night my dear," Logan said, and he cut a slice of cheese from the small wheel for them each.

If the company had failed to produce the desired results, the day, at least, could not have been more preferable. While he ate his cheese, Logan could only wonder on the mystery that was a woman's heart. He had succeeded at every aspect of his young life and he was not about to be stymied by the difficulty presented by Evelyn. However, she was, as were all women, a difficulty to be reckoned with. Time, he thought silently to himself, time will tend to her and in the end all will be as it should.

The two spoke little for the rest of the ride. They exchanged polite smiles and he even held her hand as they rode for a bit. The beauty of the countryside was enough to calm both of their spirits and it was enough for their senses to take in the sights and smells and sounds of some of the finest land ever created. Company and conversation aside, it was, a perfect day.

Chapter 21   Panic

Saturday, July 2nd, 1870

Hiram walked the long way home from Mr. Damm's that afternoon. Mr. Damm had let him off early on account of he thought that a boy his age had ought to go to town for the celebrations. Every Saturday night in the towns were times of celebrations it seemed, as it marked the day when many country folk came to town to make their trades. But the Saturday before the Fourth of July, well, Mr. Damm insisted that a young man ought not to miss it.

Mr. Damm referred to it as *"egg and daughter night,"* being that Saturdays were when the farmers brought their eggs to town to trade and their daughters in tow. A fine time to be hanging about if you were a young man, he'd thought. And no *egg and daughter night* was grander than the one directly preceding the Fourth of July as relatives from all over would descend upon their hometowns to celebrate the nation's independence.

149

Of course, Hiram cared little for the notion of a Saturday in town, but he did still have many preparations to make before he left at the end of the following week. He thought he'd see about a few of them and advance his preparations ahead of his schedule. Besides, it had donned upon him that his last week and a half of pay would be left behind anyhow, so why not take the afternoon off? His father would no doubt collect the moneys in his absence and put them down on a good drunk anyhow.

The full weight of the humid summer air bore down upon him as he traversed the rocky dirt road. At one point, Hiram wiped the sweat from his eyes and slipped into a washout from the early summer rains running down wagon ruts. Bending down, he grasped his ankle where it had been pulled as his foot had given way to the rut and cursed the unseasonable heat under his breath. There was something about those very humid Midwestern days that just seemed to make everything all the more difficult.

He must have had sweat filling his eardrums as well, or perhaps the thickness of the moisture in the air baffled the sounds around him, for when Hiram stood, he could see (and finally hear) the approaching wagon of Mr. Glenn. Most days, you could hear Mr. Glenn coming for miles it seemed, and yet there he was upon him and slowing his team as he neared.

"Ah, Mr. Wilson," Mr. Glenn exclaimed jovially. Mr. Glenn was always in such fine spirits regardless of the heat of the summer or the bone numbing cold of winter. "You have saved me a bit of a drive today, sir!"

"Have I?" Hiram replied, cocking his head in anticipation.

"You have," replied Mr. Glenn. "Let me just check in my bag here. Your house was a bit further down my list." Mr. Glenn turned in his seat and flipped open the leather flap on his mail satchel.

"I'm happy to have lessened your burden for the day then," Hiram replied, calculating the odds in his head of having run into Mr. Glenn upon the road and intercepting yet another letter from his father.

"Ah, here we are Mr. Wilson," the smiling older man said. "I have in my possession a letter of some importance I would imagine. It is addressed to one Mr. Hiram Wilson in what would appear to be the hand of a rather delicate young woman. And..." Mr. Glenn raised the letter to his nose and wafted the air above it gently with his free hand. His horses stepped back and stiffened impatiently. You'd think that they would have grown accustomed to waiting throughout his antics and conversations, but they remained restless nonetheless, "it appears to smell of the scent of flowers."

Mr. Glenn reached down and handed the letter to Hiram.

"Thank you Mr. Glenn," Hiram said, reaching up to grab it. Hiram could only stare at the letter. It had been so long since he had received one from her. It always seemed like an eternity between them, but this one was even more important to him, more urgent to read, because this one would be the last between them before they would finally be together.

"I will leave you to it then, Mr. Wilson," Mr. Glenn said, sensing the starry eyes of the young man as he stared intently at the letter before him.

"Oh yes, thank you again, Mr. Glenn. Have a fine day of it," Hiram said, not bothering to look up at the man.

"Fairly well," Mr. Glenn replied, and he raised the reigns of his impatient team in his hand and gave a quick whip into the air with them.

The team took off down the rutted dirt road and broke into a quick matched step that was a thing of beauty to any man who admired a good team. Normally, Hiram would have watched them as they rode away, admiring the perfect harmony of the pair, but he never glanced away for an instant from the business at hand. He could only see Clara, could only smell her flowery perfume; only imagine her soft voice as she sounded out his name when she had wrote the letter. The heat of the day, the horses, the bells, everything faded away except for her and her voice quietly whispering his name in the air about him.

Hiram had a system for opening her letters. It was a ritual that gave him a way of blocking out the world and focusing every part of his being upon thoughts of her. But as he stood there in the dirt road alongside a deep wagon rut with sweat dripping from his every pore and still over a mile's walk away from home, he knew that he could not wait. What's more, he could not dare risk having the fine parchment of the letter ruined, and the ink irreparably blurred by his sweat on the journey. He would have to make do to open the thing right then and there.

Hiram stepped to the side of the road, careful not to twist his ankle further in the ruts, but equally as cautious not to let the letter leave his sight lessen it evaporate or magically disappear. Stepping up from the cut of the road, he pulled himself upon the grassy bank that lined it and laid back into the weeds. For a moment, he held the letter out in front of him with the sky as its backdrop. She had such a beautiful hand. Her letters flowed from it as gracefully as words escaped her delicate lips. Everything about Clara was beautiful, everything.

Reaching into his pocket, Hiram unfolded a small knife and cut the end of the letter open. There was little need to follow such routines just then, but it had become his habit to open her letters so. Holding the thing in his hand he pressed gently down upon the paper and blew inside to open it up. Then, true to form, he smelled the perfume that wafted out of the envelope. He did not recognize the scent of this one though. He inhaled more deeply once more and closing his eyes, he tried to envision from what flower the scent had originated. Finally, she had stumped him. He did not know it, but whatever it was, it smelled incredible. Pulling the letter from its protective cover, he made note to himself to remember to ask her of it when finally they were together.

Hiram opened his eyes and glanced to the heavens as he unfolded the parchment. The clouds set against the deep blue summer sky as cut outs upon the stage of an opera house, or as a painting that hung them in place for all eternity, billowing plumes of cottony perfection suspended in mid air against a bright blue hued sky. Beams of bright sunlight radiated out from behind one and cast shining silver glimmers upon its soft edged whiteness, as if there were in that instant a brighter shade of white that had just been born for his eyes to witness.

The big billowy perfect cloud hid the sun just then, offering a brief repose from the heat of the day and Hiram imagined that it was their cloud he was viewing. That it served as yet another omen of the perfect beauty that their lives together would become. It was as if the heavens, and indeed, God himself, were smiling down upon him just then, whispering His approval into Hiram's ear of the love he had for Clara, and showing him a glimpse of the wondrous beauty that their lives together would eventually become.

Hiram smiled upwards in thanks for the cloud, for his life, for Clara, for everything. He wafted the scent of the paper across his nose once more, savoring the moment and the sights and smells of it, and began to read the words. As always, the letters were beautifully crafted, each word beginning with a capitalized letter, each letter carefully scrolled with additional curls in the most delicate of hands.

As Hiram read the words, his excitement grew. At first, he thought to console Clara; to remind her that he still loved her more than he ever had, that each day only caused his desire to be with her to grow exponentially. Then, as he passed over the words his mind struggled to comprehend their meaning, racing with dates and for a moment, he struggled to even remember what day it was just then.

"The third day of July," he read aloud, the third time he passed over the words. The third day, he thought to himself. "That's tomorrow!" he yelled aloud finally, jumping to his feet. "Tomorrow!" he exclaimed once more, looking at the letter still in disbelief.

There was too much to do. There were so many things he had yet to do before he was ready. How could he get there by the morrow? It seemed impossible to him. Indeed, it was impossible. What if he missed them? What if they were gone by the time he got there? What if...?

Hiram tucked the letter back into the envelope. As he did so, his trembling hands crumpled the paper and for a brief second, the crumpling of the paper panicked him further. For so long, he had been cherishing the scraps of parchment as his only link to Clara, that it devastated him to see realize that he had crumpled one in his carelessness. "Tomorrow," he said once more and remembered that soon, he would no longer require the letters to remind him of his love for her. Soon, he would have so much more than a pile of scented envelopes to give him joy in this life.

Tucking the letter inside of his shirt, Hiram thought about turning to head north just that instant. Everything inside of him wanted to turn and run towards her. But he remembered that back home, tucked inside of a wall were the tools he would require to make it possible. Every possession that he held dear was buried inside of that wall in the wood shed. Every penny he had to his name was there too, and every letter he had ever received from her. He'd want those letters too, if not as a reminder of a time when they served as his only hope, his singular source of inspiration, but also as a legacy that their grandchildren would read one day.

Chariton, Iowa was some distant far away place to him. The sixty or so miles that spread out between him and there was an unfathomable distance to a young man who had traveled beyond his boundaries only in company, to visit an aunt in Illinois. For as much as Hiram desired to run in that direction just then, he knew that he would never make it without money, and that the two miles or so that it would be out of his way, would be of little consequence in the grand scheme of such a journey.

Turning about, Hiram leaped on to the dirt road and ran toward his home as fast as his feet and young body could carry him. As he ran, for as much as the excitement and fear filled his spirit, and for as much as the moment of their reunion was upon him, Hiram could not help but feel that with each step, with each giant leap that he ran, that Clara, somehow, was getting further and further out of his grasp. Deep inside of Hiram, in the depths of his very soul, a panic washed over him unlike anything he had ever known and he knew just then, that despite it all, that he would never be with her again. Still with everything in him, Hiram ran.

Chapter 22   The Journey

Clara Smith looked out across the Iowa plains with mixed joy in her heart. For as much as each turn of the carriage wheel drew them closer to Chariton and Hiram, it also pulled her steadily away from her father. She had always adored her father.

Everyone said that Russell Smith was too old to make such a journey; too old to settle anew in the wilds of Nebraska, but he had an adventurous spirit and Clara knew that he would fare as well as any of them. He had watched from the comfort of their family farm in Illinois as the wagon trains rolled past on their journeys west for decades. His own inherited spread of fertile soil and growing children at home had always held him at bay though. Finally, with all of them grown and gone except for Clara and sons of age to make his land their own, he decided it time to go, lessen he live to be a hundred only to find himself trapped in a helpless body and a mire of his own regrets.

Soon after they had set about, he had discovered that the wagons which pulled their belongings were painfully slow and made but few miles of a day with their heavy burdens. He was unsatisfied with the pace of them and left them to his hired hands to drive. The family, Clara and her mother and himself, would never make the wedding of his oldest daughter if they did not go on ahead, so he opted to purchase a carriage for them instead.

They were no typical pioneers of roaming vagabonds with only their dreams and a few casks of flour to make the journey with. Rather, they were a well established family who could afford the comforts that lesser lots could only dream of. The wagons may not even make it to Nebraska by winter at their current pace, but it was of little consequence to an aging man with a purse full of coin and the dream of starting life anew.

Clara, too, had found the wagons to be painfully slow and the most uncomfortable contraptions ever designed by man. It was better on most days to simply get out and walk, lessen your bones be shaken to pieces by the lumbering vibrations of the slow moving behemoths. The carriage however, was a wonderful way to view the grassy plains and the fertile river valleys. It moved along at a fine pace, and the roads were dry and mostly quite well maintained in the eastern portions of Iowa.

For as much as she had come to think of Iowa as a wild country, quite the opposite seemed to be true. All along their journey, albeit along a well established roadway, they encountered farms and houses and towns of every sort. They were never for want of stores or liveries or inns where a hot meal could be procured. All in all, it had been a wonderful trip as they approached the Chariton River Valley.

There was only the sadness in her heart that she would soon be leaving Papa behind. He was such a good man, really. Her mother was good too, but she had never taken to her as she had her father. She wished that somehow, she could be with both of the men that she loved, but the pull of a woman inside of her to the man that she would marry was too strong to ignore. It is the primordial, biological pull that draws every girl away from her father eventually. The need to find a man cast in the same image, to love and to cherish her as she had been by him, and to make their own way together through the wilds of the world. She knew it too, but still, it gave her a heavy heart.

As they crested a hill, the Chariton River Valley spread out before them like a picture from a postcard. It was truly a beautiful place. The tall grasses of the prairies relented in their seemingly endless advance to the lush hues of thick greenery that the foliage of thousands of hundred year old oaks and cottonwoods provided. Throughout the valley and ascending the hill before them, plumes of white smoke from hundreds of summer kitchens and smokehouses puffed into the clear blue sky.

The mixture of burning oaks and hickories and smoking meats and cut grass of nearby farms filled the air with a scent that seemed almost heavenly to the weary travelers. Clara closed her eyes and inhaled deeply. What a magnificent place this Iowa was, she had thought to herself. Somewhere upwind from her the juices of scores of sausages perspired on their casings and mixed with the sweet smoke of hickory and apple woods before finally departing through a vent. The smoke, heavily laden with scents and moisture, drifted through the air until settling upon the senses of nearby travelers, beckoning them forward.

As Chariton proper spread out before them, it proved to advertise itself to the senses of weary travelers. It was not as crowded as their towns in Illinois. Indeed, a city block might only be home to as many as five and as little one house, giving each room for ample gardens and outbuildings, summer kitchens and even chicken lots. Some had small barnyards as well with cattle or sheep or horses or a mixture of the above. Everywhere, it seemed, there was construction occurring with fresh hewn planks all about them that had not yet begun to grey in the elements.

Adding to the excitement of having finally arrived, Clara was taken aback by the sheer number of people about. Every street seemed to be brimming with wagons and horses and people out walking in twos and fours. She had no way of knowing that the town was not always so boisterous. It had not donned upon her that it was due to the day, being the Saturday prior to the Fourth of July, and the people had come for miles to visit friends and relatives and to begin the festivities that were set to commence.

Clara scanned the crowd carefully. She looked into the eyes of each stranger as they passed. She turned her head to see the faces of every man in hopes that she might see *him*. Somewhere, in the crowd she hoped to find Hiram Wilson, the man that she was soon to marry. When one boy looked similar to Hiram with a slight frame and fair hair glistening in the sunshine, she even felt her heart begin to beat with excitement in her chest. Her face showed dark hues of red when she turned about to discover her mother staring oddly at her too. After that, she tried to look only out of the corner of her eyes as they advanced into the town of Chariton and the crowds only increased in density.

Passing through a patch of timber, the road emerged alongside a small lake. People stood about its banks too. Women with parasols talked to one another about the weather while boys sat fishing and men walked in the shallows pulling a seine net. Clara hoped that she and Hiram might one day settle near a river or a lake or the like. She always loved the water. Not to swim in it or anything, but rather, just to watch it, to look at it as it flowed by or glistened in the sun or rolled heavy with a strong wind. There was something mystical about water that moved her deeply, and she could imagine her and Hiram one day resting along some distant shore, holding one another close.

Before they arrived at the water, the buggy turned and headed toward the main thoroughfare. Ahead, she could see the tall brick structure that was the courthouse and the buggy turned toward it. They had missed their mark it seemed, since they had almost gone full circle, but as they neared the bustling town square, the buggy slowed to a halt. Outside of the grand two and a half-story structure hung a small sign that read, 'The Harris Inn'. Finally, they had arrived.

Chapter 23 Homecoming

Hiram Wilson ran down the lane that led to his father's farm. His body was dripping in sweat, his heart raced from the panic of being late for the most important day of his life. Entering the lane, he slowed to a jog and looked up at the elm trees that lined one side of it. They stood silently, the leaves seemingly drooping in a vein attempt to curl underneath their own individual shade for cover and hide from the sweltering heat of the mid-summer sun. From winter the trees had seemingly transformed from the foreboding stags of warning, to sad, poorly clad sentinels of distress that simply marked the entrance to a place that you'd rather not visit.

For as much as the trees lacked in foliage and shade, the house and outbuildings lacked in white wash and the yard had no sings of life, or a woman's touch. It appeared very much to be the home of a drunkard, or some other form of lazy cast about whose only purpose was to sit idly and watch as the world went to hell all about him.

161

Weeds grew up along every structure as tall as a man's waist, and Hiram noticed only then, that you could barely mark the corrals near the barn any more as they had grown into a solid patch of overgrown brambles and milkweeds. In the fields, the cattle grazed aimlessly and the portion of the farm that had once been utilized for crops grew smaller and smaller each year as the amount of seed his father could procure reduced with his shrinking ability to get credit from anyone.

It was, Hiram concluded, a place that time itself would very soon forget. If he returned here in a decade, he wondered if there would be anything left at all. It already looked the part of an abandoned homestead and it was still very much resided in. Whatever the case might be in ten years, Hiram only knew that it was a place best left behind. There was nothing there for *him* any more save a jar stuffed with money and letters from Clara. Once he had those two handfuls of treasure, he could walk away from the place, and the man who called it his home, and never look back at either of them.

Hiram had no way of knowing whether the old man was home or not. So, he quietly opened the door of the woodshed, just in case the old drunk still lurked inside of the house. As he opened the door, he looked at his plank in the wall. Indeed, every bit of caulking was gone now and he could see plain as day that the wall had a breach in it.

Careful not to let it fall to the floor, Hiram removed the plank and set it on to the floor. Behind the board, upon shelves that he himself had constructed, and where the little jars containing his treasures, and the boxes full of letters and papers, and his tiny surplus of foodstuffs...were all gone; all of it. The emptiness of the space screamed out at him and horror coursed through his veins causing every muscle in his body to weaken and rebel to the point of nearly causing him to collapse.

PSSSSHHHHTTTT! The sound settled in his ear even before he felt the sting of his father's thick leather razor strop upon his back. As Hiram arched his back in pain, the next blow landed upon his body and then the next.

"You God damned liar!" the words rang out inside of his injured ear as another blow caught his shoulder and the back of his head, "you thief!"

Hiram turned, with his arms covering his head, to face his father, who was obviously well on his way to another drunk and red with anger. The next blow caught the top of his head with the twice thick end of the strop and Hiram felt his knees begin to buckle out from under his own weight.

"Where are my things?" Hiram demanded. Another blow wrapped around his arm and landed alongside his still painful burnt face.

"You have no things, you bastard!" the older man screamed with the ferocity of a rabid civet cat, a ferocity that even Hiram had seldom bore witness to. "I feed you and clothe you and give you a roof over your head and a purpose in your miserable life only to have you steal the very bread from my table!" Elias screamed, delivering more blows with the razor strop.

Hiram pushed his way out of the corner of the woodshed and turned to face his attacker. "Where are my God damned things?!" he demanded once more.

"I ought to kill you, you worthless bastard! You're no son of mine!" the older man shouted as he delivered another blow with the strop.

The heavy end swung round his arm once again and this time caught his burnt ear with a corner. He felt the sting traverse deep inside of his head and the burning as the scab burst open and exposed the delicate skin underneath to the sting of salty sweat and the elements. Hiram had finally had enough.

Stepping in, he caught the next blow as it landed and ripped the razor strop from his father's hands. The old man continued to curse him and try to strike at him, but the tides had turned as Hiram struck him again and again. Elias backed into the same corner and folded himself into a ball at Hiram's feet.

"Where are my things?" Hiram demanded once more. As the razor strop fell from his hand, he began to kick the ball of human flesh that was curled up before him. He delivered blow after blow with his boots until the cursing, and then even the murmurs and whimpers ceased. He could not say how long he stood there kicking him or how many blows he had delivered. Hiram only knew that when he finally had stopped, the limp bag of bones and human flesh that was his own father, had slumped to the floor at his feet.

Whether he was dead or alive, Hiram could not tell, and he cared little in either event. He stepped outside of the shed and into the sweltering sun, turning to lock the door behind him. If he was not yet dead, the old man would probably die in that box, he'd thought. The same box that he had locked Hiram in for days on end on so many occasions would mark a fitting resting place, Hiram reckoned.

As he walked away toward the cabin, he noticed the swish of a tail around the corner and his heart sank even further into his belly. His father's horse was saddled and had the look of being ridden already, dark with sweat. That meant that there was no use of even looking for the money. He had already been to town in Hiram's absence. Two fresh bottles of whiskey in the saddle bags only confirmed his suspicions.

"God damn it," Hiram said aloud as he mounted the horse. "God damn it," he said desperately as he rode down the lane and glanced up once more at the dreary elms before riding away.

Chapter 24   Chicken

Sheriff Lyman looked into the steam that poured out of the dinner pail with mild enthusiasm and winced at the sight of the chicken. He had purchased two hundred fryers late that winter and they turned out to be the stringiest birds to ever have disgraced a chicken coop. Even their flavor seemed off to him.

"Thank you boys," he said, looking up from the pail of fried chicken his sons had just delivered to him straight from the kitchen at home. He then set the pail on his desk.

"Aren't you going to eat, Pa?" Sol asked, casting a worried look to Jacob. Their Pa was always a very big eater as of an evening. Whenever he worked late and hadn't shown for supper, their mother would hurriedly pack a piping hot dinner pail for him and have one of the boys rush it to the courthouse. As the Independence Day crowds had begun to amass in town, both boys had come to the square on that particular evening.

"I'll eat it later on, I reckon," Gaylord replied, looking back toward the pail on the desk. He had no intention of ever eating it though. Even the smell repulsed him after choking down the offensive fowl several times a week and with the knowledge that he'd be forced to do so at home on at least a hundred more occasions.

It might not have been such an issue, but he'd argued to buy the birds to begin with. Bella had stood there and said point blank to him, "What if they are not good eaters? To buy so many seems almost foolish."

"I think I know how to judge a chicken, Bella," he recalled having said with a painful clarity. To her credit, she had never said a word against them and the boys seemed not to have noticed either. But *she* knew and Gaylord knew that *she* knew. Even while she had never so much as said a word, Gaylord heard, or rather, ate, his words every single time he chewed into another bite of the things. And it seemed that she was serving her revenge with each plate and pail full.

"So, what are you boys up to?" Gaylord inquired, turning his thoughts away from the chicken finally.

"We just thought we'd come to town and see who all is about," Jacob replied.

"Well," Sheriff Lyman replied, "I have heard reports of more than one young lady about. Just don't either of you go causing any trouble. At least not while I am on duty," he added with a smirk.

"We can't cause any trouble anyhow, Pa," Jacob said. "Sol has confided that he intends to be a lawman one day."

"Jacob," Sol grimaced at his older brother for having betrayed a confidence.

"Is that a fact?" Gaylord asked, looking at the younger of his two sons and shaking his head affirmatively.

"I only said that I was thinking of it," Sol replied sheepishly.

"I believe that you'd make a fine lawman," Gaylord said.

"Really, Pa? I thought you'd be upset since you are quitting the job," Sol's eyes widened in response to the unexpectedly positive affirmation from his father.

"Sol," the Sheriff replied. "I am quitting because it is the right thing for me to do. I need to spend more time with you boys and your mother. I have much to do on the farm as well and at the house. But that is what is right for me. What is right for you is for you to decide and it so happens that you would make a fine lawman if you have a mind to do it."

"Will you teach me how to shoot proper and such then Pa?" Sol asked.

Gaylord thought on it and was perplexed that he had asked such a thing. Had he really not ever taught them how to handle a pistol? Had he been so derelict in his fatherly duties that the almost grown sons of a sheriff did not know how to care for and draw a pistol? Gaylord sighed deeply and exhaled, feeling the old sickness return to the pit of his stomach. It was the familiar feeling of a man who had not lived up to his own promises, not held his end of any bargain with his sons.

"Of course I will teach you son," he replied shamefully.

"When?" Sol inquired. "Can we do it this evening?"

"No," Gaylord replied. "I have much to do and the county is still depending upon me. Let me get through the holiday celebrations and I will make time for it, son. I promise. I'll show you some then, and when I have quit the post in the fall, I will teach you everything a lawman needs to know."

"Okay, Pa," Sol said with some disappointment, but with an earnest appreciation in his tone still.

With that the boys turned to depart and haunt the Chariton streets with the other boys.

"Sol?" Gaylord called after him.

"Yes sir?" the boy turned back to him.

"You will make a fine lawman," Gaylord said.

"Thank you, Pa," he smiled at him and then walked out.

Gaylord exhaled. He really would make a fine lawman, he thought. He has the personality for it. He wished that he didn't have to put him off though. He'd failed them enough and he wished that he could start showing then and there that things were going to be different between them. He wished that he could spend the rest of the night showing his son how to draw a pistol and how to clean it, and how to file just a bit of metal off the thing to make it slide out of the holster faster when you needed it. Soon, he thought to himself. It'll all be different pretty soon boys. I promise.

"Boys!" he called after them, hurriedly running to the door.

"Yes sir?" Sol called back as the two stood outside.

"I'm sorry," he said. "I lied to you both."

"Pa?" Sol looked at him confused.

"I'm not going eat the chicken at all," he said. "It is terrible chicken."

"We know, Pa," Sol replied nonchalantly, and the two turned and walked away.

As Gaylord walked into his office, he realized that the boys had known it all along and had sat and quietly chewed through every bite, even asking their mother for seconds without ever saying a word to them. In that instant, he had never been prouder of the men they had become. Soon boys, he thought again. I'll make it all up to you.

Chapter 25   Reunion

Walking up the steps of the Inn, Clara thought that she might be walking into a home back east of some wealthy friend of Papa's. The house was the largest one in view and only two other homes were located on the same block. The trees surrounding it had considerable size as well and marked the yard of some well established persons who had been in Iowa for a good while. For there were only two sorts of yard trees really; those that had been recently planted to conform to the relatively recent order of the streets and homes, and those mighty oaks and elms and hickories that had been in their places long before anyone had ever thought of this place called Chariton. Still, the trees in the yards around and adjacent to the Inn were somewhere in between.

The wooden steps and the porch that surrounded the front and sides of the home were painted a shiny gray while the rest of the two and a half story structure was a brilliant white (in stark contrast to the vast majority of homes and businesses which had been left in their natural state.) All around them buildings and homes shone somewhere between freshly hewn-wood-yellow and dark, weather-worn-dull-gray. But the Harris Inn and the other homes on the block were as if someone had picked up the fanciest, shiniest homes from back in Illinois and dropped them in the midst of a growing frontier boom town.

As they made their way over the crest of the stairs leading up to the porch, Clara heard the screen door creak open and a stout old woman appeared wearing an apron and a warm smile.

"Greetings strangers," the old woman said, "and welcome to the Harris Inn. I gather that you must be the Smiths?"

"We are," Clara's father replied.

"I have heard so much about you. I am Mrs. Harris," she replied with a smile. "There is coffee in the parlor. Please go inside and make yourselves at home. I shall have the neighbor boy tend to your bags. And would you like your animals and buggy stabled?"

"Indeed, we would," Mr. Smith replied as they entered the home and were greeted by a grand staircase that wound around above their heads in the open space that filled the entry way.

"I shall see to it then. The nearest livery is only a block away, but I recommend going the extra two blocks to the north end of town. The man there is all the kinder to the stock," Mrs. Harris stated.

"That will be fine," he said. "Thank you."

"The parlor is just in there. I shall call on Evelyn, I mean...Mrs. Bates," she corrected herself, forgetting her manners in the midst of her familiarity.

"Thank you so much Mrs. Harris," Mrs. Smith said smiling. "Evelyn has spoke well of you, and often, in her letters. And thank you for your kindness to her. It does a mother's heart good to know that her daughter has someone like you watching out for her," she said. Recognizing the older woman was distraught by her faux pas, she sought to give her comfort her with familiarities of her own.

"Was no kindness, Ma'am," the woman replied, "your daughter and grandson have been one of the great joys of this old woman's heart. I have been blessed to have them in my home. You have done well and raised yourself a fine young lady," she said.

"Thank you," Mrs. Smith replied and gave the old woman a knowing, bright eyed smile as the family shuffled in to find comfort in the parlor.

"I shall see to your things now and return shortly to show you to your rooms," Mrs. Harris said as she disappeared up the staircase.

Clara sat down on a couch beside her mother while Papa poured them each a cup of coffee before sitting in a chair beside them. It was fine coffee and Clara felt as though she was sitting upon a plush cloud after riding in the bumpy carriage for so many days. Even with the plushest of padding on the carriage seats, as the hours had turned into days, the firmness of the wooden plank underneath caused aching tenderness upon one's bottom.

As they let out a collective sigh of relief and began to let their bodies relax, Evelyn walked into the room. She was even more beautiful than Clara had remembered her. Evelyn wore a long flowing lavender dress with off-white lace surrounding every opening. Her locks of shiny black hair were perfectly arranged and her effortless smile cast a warm hue of joy throughout the parlor.

The entire family leaped from their repose to embrace her. Even long after Papa and the girls' mother had returned to their seats, Clara and Evelyn stood in the doorway of the parlor holding one another and crying.

For as much as they'd had several other siblings and as great as their difference in age, Evelyn had always been the closest in Clara's heart. Indeed, she looked at her in the light of somewhere between an older sister and a second mother who she adored with love and reverence.

"Clara, let your sister breathe," Papa said. And finally, she relinquished her grip and settled back into her chair.

Evelyn stood for a moment and wiped the tears away from her cheeks with her kerchief. Her face powder had mingled with the moisture of her tears, forming little balls of silken colored goop near her eyes.

"I must look a fright," she said and flashed an embarrassed smile over her kerchief.

"You look beautiful as the day you were born," her mother replied warmly.

"How was your journey?" Evelyn inquired as she found a chair beside Papa's and turned it so they would all be in full view, and she of them.

With that, Papa started in on his long version of the events of how they had started with the wagons but found them cumbersome and too slow for his schedule and his patience. He then recounted almost every mile and every cloud they had encountered along the way. Clara loved her Papa with all of her young heart, but still, he had a way of telling a thing that bored her terribly. She had even come to cringe whenever anyone would ask him such an open ended question because she knew well what the result would be.

Their mother was beginning to fall asleep as he spoke and was only jostled back to life when Mrs. Harris finally entered the parlor.

"Your rooms are ready," she announced. "And there is hot water waiting for you in the basin upstairs." Mrs. Harris was uncertain based on Evelyn's instructions, exactly when her new guests would arrive. But in anticipation of such important guests, she had maintained a very large extra kettle in the outdoor kitchen behind the residence of hot water for just the occasion.

"Oh, bless you, Mrs. Harris," their mother said wearily as she rose slowly from the couch, feeling her age in the creaks of her aching joints and muscles.

"I reckon we had best clean ourselves then, and let your mother rest," Papa announced and rose to follow Mrs. Harris to the finest room in the Inn that had once served as her very own master bedroom.

Clara remained seated on her chair as the others departed and waited as Evelyn walked her parents to the doorway and gave them each a kiss.

"Would you fancy a walk?" Evelyn said, turning around to Clara.

"Yes. I would fancy it greatly," Clara replied joyfully.

As Clara and Evelyn went along the crowded planked walkways lining the downtown Chariton businesses, Evelyn spoke of Mr. Logan and his interests and of each business they encountered along the way.

Almost everyone in the busy street seemed to know her too, and wished her well. Those gentlemen who did not know her would stare at her as if she were a beautiful sunrise and tip their hat in reverence. Clara was so proud to call her a sister. For as much as Evelyn seemed not to notice in her own grace, Clara was in awe of her.

She wished that she could tell her about their plans and all about Hiram, but how could she? Clara wondered to herself if she could entrust such knowledge to anyone. But truly, if there were anyone she *could* tell, it was Evelyn. What would she think of her? Would she tell Papa? Such were the thoughts that entertained her mind as yet another young man approached them on the crowded Chariton walkway.

After nearly an hour and so many people wishing Evelyn a good afternoon and the like, Clara scarcely paid any notice to the young man as he neared them. When she did look up, she found a tall, handsome man who was probably too cock sure of himself to know that Evelyn was far too old for him, and far too beautiful as well.

"Beautiful day isn't it ladies?" the young man asked.

"It is quite lovely," Evelyn replied.

"Made all the more beautiful by your presence," the shameless courtier replied.

Clara rolled her eyes, but Evelyn only smiled at him graciously and thanked him for his kind words.

"No ma'am," he replied, "I mean you are very beautiful, Mrs. Bates," he said sheepishly. "But I was speaking to the young lady by your side."

"Ah," Evelyn answered with a nod of her head. "You are quite right. She is very beautiful. Mr. Jacob Lyman," Evelyn said, "I present to you my sister, Ms. Clara Smith, formerly of Illinois."

"It is a great pleasure to make your acquaintance, Ms. Smith," Jacob bowed his head as if to kiss her hand, but stopped short and paused there momentarily, feeling the softness of her tiny hand in his own.

"Thank you," Clara replied, still in a bit of shock at what had just transpired. He *was* a very handsome young man after all, and very tall as well. She suddenly felt beside herself for not having cleaned the road from her dress or fixed her hair or...*anything*. As her face blushed mildly, she took a small step away from him so that he might not notice every flaw of her tattered appearance.

"Would you do me the honor of walking with me about the city tomorrow?" he asked.

"Mr. Lyman," Evelyn interjected, "I had no idea you had it in you to call upon every young lady you met in such a fashion."

"Neither did I, Mrs. Bates," he replied sheepishly, "but as I stood there on yonder porch I was just sort of struck by this beautiful young woman. I have never felt so compelled in all of my living days. So, would you...walk with me?" he looked at Clara once again.

"I'm sorry," Clara replied, "I just..."

"She would be honored," Evelyn said, shooting her a quick, almost imperceptible wink. "You may come to call at the Inn for her around four o'clock tomorrow," Evelyn said in a rather serious tone, as if she were conducting a business deal and had just finalized the terms of the thing.

"Thank you kindly, ma'am," Jacob replied. "I shall see you in the morrow then, Ms. Smith," he said smiling and bowing his head to her. He might have tipped his hat as well had it not been clutched tightly in his grip throughout the entire exchange.

"There," Evelyn said, as he walked away. "Now you've made your first impression upon Chariton, Iowa, dear sister, and we can return to the Inn so you that you might wash the road off of you."

"You don't understand," Clara replied nervously. Clearly, she was going to have to tell her sister everything so she would stop trying to tend the affairs of marrying her off.

"Hold on a moment," Evelyn replied. "Oh, Mr. Lyman!" she called after the boy just as he was about to disappear into the crowd before them. Turning immediately about, he ran back to the women where they remained on the walkway in front of the dry goods store.

"Yes?" he said, breathing heavily.

"When you come to call, please do so for a Mr. Smith," she said.

"Mr. Smith?" he asked with a confused look upon his face and then cast the same look to Clara.

"Yes, it is our...I mean, Ms. Smith's father and I am certain that he will require a word with you before your walk," she said, holding back her smile.

"Yes ma'am, of course," he replied, slightly less enthusiastic than he had been before, but still apparently undeterred. "I shall do just that then," he said, tipping his hat once more before departing.

As the sisters walked back to the Inn, Clara let loose of everything she had been holding in her own secretive heart for so long. She told Evelyn about how she had fallen madly in love with Hiram Wilson and about how they had been exchanging letters for such a time and even about their plans for the future. It was hard to begin, but once Clara started the telling of the thing, it burst forth as the water from a dynamited beaver dam.

"...and that is why I simply cannot walk with that boy tomorrow," Clara finally finished.

Stopping on the walk in front of the Inn, Evelyn turned to face her sister. She grasped her by the shoulders and Clara winced at what motherly scolding might be about to commence.

"You *will* walk with him tomorrow," she said. "He is from very fine stock here, and very handsome to boot," she said. "And as for this Hiram Wilson business," she said, looking Clara directly in the eyes as she spoke. "If I may teach you one thing that I have learned about being a woman through all of my experiences...it is that it is *always* good to have options." And she smiled at her sister quickly before turning to head up the stairs and inside the Inn.

Clara was relieved at the talk and the tone that Evelyn had taken with her. More than ever, she felt a bond with her elder sibling of the likes that she had never experienced with anyone before. Clara knew then, at that very moment, that she could tell her sister anything. That finally, she would never again be alone in the world when it came to matters of the heart too sensitive for her father's ears and too delicate for her mother's understanding.

As Evelyn raised her dress slightly and ascended the stairs, Clara could only stand looking at her in awe. What an amazing woman her sister truly was. She was beautiful and graceful and elegant to be certain, but more than that, she was inspiring.

"Aren't you coming, dear?" Evelyn paused at the top of the stairs and stood upon the porch of the grand house that was the Inn. She was the quintessential modern woman. The perfect picture of what a woman ought to be. Standing there, in such perfection, Evelyn cast an aura about her that Clara soaked in as if rays from a warm morning sun. But even with all of that, Evelyn was something much more as well. To Clara, she was...a sister.

"You are truly beautiful," Clara replied.

"As are you sister," Evelyn replied, "as are you. Now come along inside dear. There is someone who should be up from his nap that I would like very much to reacquaint you with."

"Is it little Ellis?" Clara asked excitedly, having nearly forgotten about her nephew through it all.

"It is," Evelyn smiled back at her.

And the two disappeared hurriedly into the Inn, letting the screen door slam in their wake as if small children had just

180

clamored inside. The house was full of laughter and the giggling of girls and somewhere in or near the kitchen, old Mrs. Harris stood smiling and rejoicing to have her house sound like a home again.

Chapter 26 Hiram's Ride

Hiram Wilson rolled over in the sandy dirt of the river bank where he had laid the night before and spit the sand off of his lips. Some time during the night, he had rolled off of the saddle that he had used as a pillow.

He had ridden into the darkness the night before until his horse would go no further. Already having been ridden several miles by his father that day, the old horse could go no more. It had been just as well anyhow as even Hiram had been on the brink of collapse.

They had camped along the banks of a small wooded river he had encountered along the road and Hiram reckoned it to be well on the Iowa side of the border. With no houses or lights in sight of any sort, it had seemed a safe place to stop and bed for the night. His horse, safely hobbled to a chunk of log, was standing in the grass along the edge of the timber, thoughtlessly grazing.

That night, Hiram had dreamed that the horse had gone home and that he had missed getting to Clara, so it was of considerable relief to him to see it still standing there. Rising, Hiram staggered down to the river and throwing off his clothes, he dove into the warm, dark water.

It would have been nice if the water had been a bit cooler. It was almost difficult to feel the difference upon his flesh between the sticky dry sweat and sand that had coated his skin and the warm, dirty, slow flowing water of the river. But it was wet and as he rinsed his body with his hand, it offered a pleasant relief from sweat and sand, even if it only came in the form of another sort of dirt.

Feeling the stiffness in his neck and joints, Hiram passed his hand over his shoulder and up through his hair. He winced and let loose a profane retort to the pain as he passed over his ear that had been, in recent days, burnt and whipped, scabbed and broken, and scabbed again. He was joyous only that he had no mirrored glass about to see for himself how wretched he must appear to the world. If he could see himself, he knew that he would never be able to face her. As it was, he could try to forget just long enough to steal her away. Clara would make some remarks about his condition and the two would ride away anyhow. In time, his wounds would heal and all would be as it should.

He looked about for anything along the river's edge that might serve as a breakfast. The growling in his gut only worsened as he swallowed a drink of water from the river. In a hole beside the shore, he moved slowly upon some fish that rested near the bottom but as he dove to catch one, they only darted safely out of his reach and came to rest again. This went on similarly for three or four attempts before he finally gave up on the idea of trying to catch one and emerged from the river empty handed and empty bellied.

Whatever suffering had consumed him, and whatever trials awaited him, he'd thought, they were worthy of the outcome. Finally, regardless of it all, he was riding to his beloved Clara. As he saddled his horse and ignored the protests of his grumbling stomach, Hiram filled his mind with thoughts of *her*. He could see her now, standing before him in some long, flowing summer dress and smelling of fresh flowers. Her smile would wash away every worry that he had ever known in this life. When he finally took her into his arms, the world as he knew it would cease to exist. It would be a new world for him where right always trumped wrong. Finally, they would be free to make their own way together, living, loving, laughing and enjoying the great adventure that would be their life.

"I am coming for you, Clara," he said aloud as he rode, smiling for the first time that he could recall as of late. "I am finally coming for you."

All throughout that Sunday it was all that Hiram could do not to kick the beast in the sides and run the animal until it dropped. The pace was killing him to know that Clara was only some fifty or sixty miles away. The horse though, was too old to run for any length. He knew that it would make far better time in the long run to maintain a steady walk than to even attempt a gallop for a short distance. Besides wearing the animal out, a good run in the summer heat might well have killed her altogether, and then where would he be? He would be counting off days or weeks instead of hours between them, that's where. No. It was best to simply keep walking off the miles and steadily closing the gap between them.

All through that Sunday as he rode, Hiram struggled to stave off his hunger. The prairie winds did not come to him that day and as the miles wore on, the heat of the sun began to slump him into his saddle as if it were slowly melting the bones within his body that held him erect. Even the leaves of the tallest trees failed to tremble to any hint of a breeze.

As the sun finally began to lower itself in the sky, Hiram found himself barely awake in his saddle. He had never ridden so far in a single day in all of his life. Clara or no, he could simply travel no further. He would rest for awhile, he thought to himself, and then set out after dark again and ride through the rest of the night.

It was a tough decision to make to stop so early and lose the many hours of gentle daylight that the Iowa summer had to offer, but they needed the break, so he assured himself that they'd make up for it later.

As Hiram unsaddled the horse, the gods or fate or something intervened into his dire situation. As if dropped from heaven above, plucked from the roost of God himself and delivered unto him, a chicken emerged from the underbrush of the small creek bottom and gave a cluck to ensure that his weary eyes had not deceived him.

The hours he'd intended for rest were instead expended to construct a fire. In his haste, he had failed to secure a single match. By the time he was able to make a flame, darkness had set upon him. By the time he had finished every morsel of the tough old bird, sleep would wait no more. And Hiram slept.

Chapter 27   The Walk

The next day at promptly ten minutes to four in the afternoon, a young Jacob Lyman could be seen pacing the walk in front of the Harris Inn. His hair was neatly greased and combed. His pants were pressed and sharp, and his jacket was as free of hair and lint as the thing had ever been since the day that his mother had sewn it for him.

The screened door of the porch leading into the Inn swung open and Evelyn stuck her head out. "If you are going to simply pace out there, you'd just as well come and do it in the parlor while you wait," she said before disappearing back inside. She was having more fun with the boy than she ever might have imagined.

Jacob entered the Inn and followed her into the parlor where her entire family sat, having a coffee with Mrs. Harris. The occupants of the room all turned and stared at him, and Jacob stood frozen and speechless in the doorway.

"If that hat were a kitten, you'd have choked the life out of it," Mr. Smith said to him. "Let loose your grip boy, and come in."

Jacob felt the blood rush to his cheeks and he stepped awkwardly into the room, making every effort not to fidget with his hat. Looking to Clara, he smiled uncomfortably and then swallowed hard before attempting to speak.

"Good afternoon, sir," he said nervously to Mr. Smith. "My name is Jacob Lyman and I have come to call upon your daughter, if it pleases you."

Clara's father stood and eyed the young man carefully. He looked him all the way to his shoes, then slowly back up to his face. "You look a little young to be calling on my daughter Evelyn," he said teasing.

"Papa!" Clara scolded, embarrassed at the harassment she was witnessing.

The elder Smith only smiled broadly at her and then cast a look in the way of Evelyn who shared in the delight of the moment far more than the rest. For as much as Evelyn and Papa were enjoying themselves and Clara had liked to die of humiliation, their mother sat quietly, and only appeared annoyed by the lot of them.

"No, sir," Jacob replied. "I am here to call on Clara. I should like to take her for a walk around the square and show her Chariton."

"Hmmm," Mr. Smith replied, turning serious once more. "I would not be inclined to entertain such a request being in a town that is strange to me," he said, watching as the expression in Jacob's face altered from tension to despair. "However," the older man continued, "Evelyn has informed me that you are the son of the local sheriff and a top employee of her fiancé, Mr. Logan."

"That is correct, sir," Jacob said, glancing back up from his shoes as his fortune seemingly shifted for the better.

"In that case," Mr. Smith continued, "I shall expect you to be on your finest behavior then and representative of the town and its best."

"Yes sir," Jacob replied. "I will, sir."

"And you shall see to the protection of my daughter as if she were your own blood?" Mr. Smith queried.

"You may be certain of it sir," Jacob replied anxiously.

"Then yes," Clara's father finally smiled directly at Jacob, "you may take Clara for a walk. But you are to stay on or near the square and well in public view. And she is to be returned by you to the Inn prior to nine o'clock this evening."

"Of course," Jacob replied. "You will not regret this, sir. Thank you," he said.

"Then, Mr. Jacob Lyman," Mr. Smith said in a quite formal tone, "I present to you my youngest daughter, Ms. Clara Smith," he said reaching for Clara's hand as she rose from the couch. The formality of it all was almost more than the young people could stand. Both of them were equally as eager to get away from the piercing eyes that had been upon them throughout the entire ordeal.

The pair started off quite slow in conversation as they walked slowly from one boarded walk to another. Jacob walked Clara to a portion of the street that had been brick paved for pedestrians to cross between two prominent businesses. The rest of the Chariton streets were still muddy from a recent mid-summer rain.

As they walked, it seemed that everyone in town knew the young man. Clara was reminded of how it had been to walk with her sister the day before. There was something very wonderful about this little town among the tall Iowa grass. The people were all friendly toward one another and Clara felt lucky to have been in the company with two of Chariton's most apparently beloved citizens in such a short span of time.

Strolling along the town square boardwalk once again, Jacob would tell her about the men who owned the businesses. It was the evening prior to the Independence Day celebration, and while businesses remained officially closed for Sunday, nearly every door was open as friends and relatives crowded in every shop for miniature reunions, and to see the latest developments of the growing city.

"It is wonderful here," Clara said. "Everyone is so very nice."

"Yes," he said. "It seems that way, doesn't it?"

"You mean everyone isn't so very nice?" she puzzled.

"No. I didn't mean to say *that,*" he replied. "It's only that not everything and everyone is always what they seem at first, that's all."

"Whatever do you mean, Jacob?" she stopped and turned to look at his face. There was something ruggedly handsome about him that she could not quite place. At the same time though, he managed to have in his eyes a sincerity that she seldom saw in a boy his age.

"The people are fine here," he said softly. "It's just..."

"Just what?" Clara asked.

"It's just that some of the finest people turn out to be disappointing once you get to know them better sometimes," he replied. "Like Mr. Logan..." he cut himself short as he remembered who was speaking to.

"Evelyn's fiancé?" she queried. "What about him?"

"Nothing," Jacob replied. "We should walk for a bit. I think the sun must be getting to me."

"Jacob," she said, grasping his arm lightly and turning him back toward her. "There is something that I should tell you."

"What is it?" he asked.

"I have a fiancé of sorts as well," she confessed. "I should not have accepted your offer to come, but Evelyn..."

"Where is he?" Jacob asked.

"He is in Missouri," Clara replied, "but he should be here soon. I wouldn't have even come and I should like to not have mentioned it, but you seem like such a nice boy. I just wanted you to know. That is all."

"Clara," Jacob looked her in the eyes and gazed deeply into them. "I've never approached anyone like this before. I don't really even know what came over me. But when I saw you yesterday, I just knew that if I let you pass without saying anything that I would regret it for the rest of my living days. I have no expectations really. I am amazed and awestruck to even be walking with you. I can't say why exactly; I mean, you truly are beautiful, but there is something else about you too. I just had to get to know you or I'd never have forgiven myself. If you marry another then so be it, but for whatever reason, I just had to."

Clara stood silently and looked into the depths of his sparkling eyes. As he spoke, his words echoed inside of her ears, but her spirit had been swimming inside of his eyes the entire time. It was as if they were transparent and she could see directly through them and inside to a warm and loving spirit. Being with him gave her such a comfort and simple pleasure that she had not known since she had last seen Hiram. She was beginning to wonder if it was possible for lightning to strike a body twice.

The two continued on their walk, and as they did, the conversation became easier. She had walked with boys before back home and never found them to be to her liking or capable of even a basic conversation. Jacob Lyman was a different sort altogether. He was handsome and smart. But he was something else as well; he was both strong and tender, both rugged and soft, both funny and serious. In short, he was everything that was good about her father, and everything she had always sought in a man of her own.

As they returned to the Inn (an hour early by Jacob's insistence), Clara could not help but wonder if it was possible to meet someone new and *know* them. It was as if she had known Jacob her entire life already. In a few short hours, she felt closer to Jacob than she felt to people she had known for years.

She loved Hiram. With all of her heart, she loved him, but here she was nonetheless, wondering how on Earth that this had come to pass. For the first time in her young life, Clara felt the burden of doubt cast a dark shadow across the otherwise perfect blue skies of her heart. In the course of but a few hours she discovered that it is possible to fall in love in an instant, in a moment, in the blink of an eye and the mingling of kindred spirits shared in an exchange of gazes during an earnest second. But too, she learned that it is possible to fall for more than one soul for different reasons.

Jacob insisted on walking her inside and delivering safely to her father as had been his request. Mr. Smith, it seemed, was so impressed by the young man having her home early and his show of respect, that he invited Jacob to join them for an engagement dinner of sorts the following evening to which he readily accepted before saying a cordial fairly well to Clara in her father's presence.

That night while the rest of the family slept, Clara paced the second story catwalk of the Inn outside of her room and watched the clouds roll slowly in, engulfing the starlit night with a coming storm. Similarly, she could not help but feel the clouds enveloping her own heart as she struggled to comprehend what had happened to her that day. She was always so certain of her love for Hiram before. She was still quite certain of it too. But what if she was meant to be with Jacob? What if her heart was leading her astray? If she chose incorrectly she could lose them both in the end.

As the storms blew in, her heart only grew heavier until a raging tempest of tumult inside of her tore at the very fabric of her being. It all came down to this. A woman spent her entire life dreaming of finding her one true love. When he arrived, if ever he did, it was up to her to know it and to seize upon the moment of opportunity. For the first time she considered the possibility that Hiram Wilson would not arrive as planned. Worst of all, for the first time, she found herself wishing that he wouldn't.

Outside, somewhere in the dark and stormy night, as the winds blew and the lightning flashed, Hiram Wilson was riding towards her.

Chapter 28   Independence Day

The Inn that day was just as Mrs. Harris would have liked it, full of life and people. She had decided to forego the speeches and events held in the courtyards that afternoon and throw a party of her own. Her son was there from up north with his wife and children. So too were the Smiths, and she had even invited the rest of the Lyman Clan, knowing full well that the Sheriff would be busy throughout the festivities.

The entire lot of them waited patiently for Clara and Evelyn to make their entrance to the back yard where Mrs. Harris had arranged the tables and food. Even the youngest girls knew that the sisters were not really getting ready. The peaks out of the second story window periodically only served to confirm the suspicion of the guests below that the girls were only waiting for the right moment to make their grand entrance. Such was the way of women of the day whether in the swankest of Chicago balls or an afternoon luncheon in Chariton, Iowa.

193

While waiting in the yard, the girls' father had the opportunity to exchange some words with Mr. Jasper Logan too. And while he would never admit it, there was something about the man that rubbed him wrong. He was a braggart for one, and Papa had always despised a braggart. Their father was no idler or drifter either. He was a man of substantial self made means. Perhaps even of more than Mr. Logan himself. Still, despite it all, Papa had never been a braggart to anyone.

Clara inspected herself in the mirror wearing the dress her sister had surprised her with. It was a beautiful flowing shade of light blue with red and pink hued floral lace all about it. It was a magnificent dress, and in the reflection she could see for the first time, a beauty within herself that was similar to that of her sister, Evelyn. She had always felt the lesser of the two in the way of beauty, being much the younger and always hearing others speak of Evelyn's handsomeness. Despite kind words from anyone, she could never see herself in the same light before that day. She was not, in her mind, as pretty as her sister still, but she felt, for perhaps the first time ever, genuinely beautiful.

The tables had been neatly arranged in a row and covered with delicate white clothe that Mrs. Harris had stitched to give it the appearance of a single twenty foot long banquet table near her garden. On the tables sat every sort of foodstuff; enough to feed twice as many souls. There were hams that had been provided by Mr. Logan and two wheels of his famous cheese. There was cold watermelon that had been on ice all morning until being cut only minutes before. There were potatoes too, mashed and baked with fresh churned butter and gravy ladles and a number of toppings and early vegetables, cut fresh from the garden that very day.

It was a feast fit for royalty and Mrs. Harris could not have been more pleased, having a yard overflowing with guests. The sounds of people chatting and children laughing and playing filled the air and swelled her old heart with a joy she had not known in a number of years.

Finally, the sound of murmured talking amongst the little crowds of guests ceased and they all began to clap as the girls finally emerged from the balcony doors. They were a sight to behold as they walked side by side down the stairs that led to the garden. It was as if a scene from some far away place and time for certainly such beauty had not been known since the grey eyed Goddess, Pallas Athena had herself stepped tender footed upon the sandy beaches of the Troad.

At least, such were the thoughts that raced through young Jacob Lyman's mind as he watched his own Greek Goddess descend the steps with her sister. Jacob stood beside Jasper Logan near the end of the stairs to take their lady's hands when they stepped to the ground. Even Jasper had clapped as the girls emerged. Jacob could only stand there, looking up at her as if she were a beautiful starlit night. Certainly, he'd thought, there has never been a more beautiful woman anywhere in the world, ever.

The girls smiled brightly and seemed to float down the stairway in perfect unison. As they made the last step, they both paused and presented their hands to their perspective suitors. It was a grand entrance for a grand party and long after the others had stopped, Mrs. Harris stood under the shade of the giant maple tree and continued to clap, wearing a smile as wide her apron.

As the guests were finally seated, they found a glass of water and buttermilk at each seat under the old tree. Jasper Logan, not being one to miss seizing upon such a moment, stood and raised his glass of buttermilk in a toast. "To the most beautiful sisters in all of Lucas County," he'd said, holding his glass high before taking a sip of it and carrying on with subsequent toasts.

Mr. Smith listened disdainfully and watched the heat roll off of the ham and potatoes. He had no use for this Logan fellow and his endless grandstanding toasts only reaffirmed that which he had already suspected. Then, glancing across the table, his eyes found young Jacob Lyman casting a similar glare of contempt at Jasper Logan. He knew he'd liked *something* about *that* young man and just then, he was certain of it.

Jacob had been sipping his buttermilk to the final toast when the two o' clock cannon fired and he nearly leapt out of his seat. The buttermilk sloshed upwards and covered the front of him and the entire table roared with laughter. It was a tradition of the day to fire the civil war relic at the top of every hour in honor of America's Independence and every shot caused Jacob to almost leap into the air like a wounded cat.

For his part, Jacob, although red with embarrassment, laughed heartily alongside the rest of the guests and Clara loved him all the more for it. How many boys of his age might well have stomped off in angry embarrassment? Jacob only laughed along with them, making it all the more enjoyable for the rest of the guests.

As the ham slowly disappeared and the heat of the day fell upon them, the guests found themselves huddled under the shade of the big tree. It was such a maple as one might mistake for a mighty oak from a distance and shaded nearly a third of Mrs. Harris' sprawling backyard. As the day wore on the chairs were only shifted occasionally to stay under the shade as the sun passed through the clear summer sky.

As the top of each new hour approached, the guests would all begin whispering some inside joke to one another. The talking would slowly get quieter and quieter until the cannon on the Chariton square finally boomed and Jacob jumped nearly out of his skin. With each booming of the relic, Clara only fell more deeply in love with the boy. He was handsome yes, but he was strong too, and had a humble way about him in everything that let Clara know of the kind softness of the heart that beat within his breast.

With the evening, Clara finally began to relax more completely. Hiram Wilson had not arrived. It was foolish of her to ever think that he would. What they'd had was a childish thing and conceived by the imagination of childish hearts. Jacob Lyman, though, was real. All throughout the day, Clara had fretted about what she would do if Hiram Wilson arrived. How could she leave Jacob standing here and ride off with a boy she'd not seen in almost two years and only knew from letters? Anyone can say nice things in letters, but here was Jacob in the flesh and blood, smart and wonderful and humble and strong and sensitive. Thank God, she'd said to herself as the sun set on another day; thank God that Hiram did not come for me.

As the fireworks began to light the night sky from the town square, Clara stood relieved and completely in love with Jacob, hand in hand by Mrs. Harris' back fence. Even as Clara stared at the sky, she felt his eyes upon her. She glanced to find Jacob staring at her all the while, apparently unmoved by the fiery explosions above them.

Jacob lightly squeezed her hand, marveling at the softness and the smallness of it in his. She did not know it, but as he looked at her in the light of each burst of fire in the sky, he was experiencing fireworks all of his own. He was as certain of it as he had ever been of anything; he was desperately in love with Clara Smith and he would never let her go.

As the couple's hearts melded into one and each breath drew them inseparably closer to one another, Hiram Wilson, half starved, thirsty, and barely upright from fatigue, rode steadily toward them.

Chapter 29   Relief

For most everyone in Chariton, Independence Day was eagerly awaited and vigorously celebrated. To a sheriff it was something very different though. For Sheriff Gaylord Lyman, it had been the last Fourth of July that he would serve as Lucas County Sheriff. He was more than a little relieved to have put the day behind him.

For a sheriff, the celebration marked the most dangerous day of the year. Hundreds of people descended upon Chariton. Some were strangers and some were old friends or relatives who had not been back in years. It meant that it was a day for settling old scores between men whose paths might not have crossed in a decade. It meant that men not accustomed to being in one another's company, would drink too much whiskey and fire their guns in the air. All too often, it also meant that before morning broke, they'd be firing their guns at each other as well.

The sun had not even begun to rise on the 5th of day of July, 1870, when Sheriff Lyman walked into the courthouse and put his boots upon his desk. With his heels dug into the edge of the old desk, he pulled the boots up on his tired feet. The Independence Day celebration had come to an abrupt and final end with a heavy, pre-dawn summer rain, pushing even the hardiest drunkards under stairways and boardwalks and out of harm's way for the night. The sheriff had made one final walk through the sleeping town in the rain and had come to the courthouse to rest and have a coffee or two.

The courthouse was a special place for him. It was not only his office, but it was the place where he went to unwind and shed the tension and mud he'd gathered while out chasing rumors of horse thieves and collecting wanted men. While most other men would be heading straight home to rest their heads upon their pillows at such an hour, Sheriff Lyman preferred to relax and breath in the comfortable safety of his office until morning broke.

Having survived the last Independence Day he'd ever work as the sheriff was no small thing. He had been dreading the day for weeks once he had made the decision to retire from the office and now it was finally in his wake. He had never been afraid of his job before that day, but with the end so near in his sights, an uneasy feeling had come over him. For as much as he looked forward to being with his family soon, he knew he'd wasted so many days between that one and the day in the Nebraska Territory when he had promised to live better if only he could get back alive. He hadn't lived better, of course, and as the day approached when he intended to finally keep his promise, he was nagged by the feeling that fate was going to pay him visit.

But fate had not arrived that Independence Day in 1870 and sitting in his office, he finally let loose a deep breath of relief. Finally, he could relax and look forward to living the life he had owed it to his family, himself, and four dead men, to live all along. Fate had given him a second chance to make it all even and he was genuinely grateful to be sitting there alive, drinking stale coffee and looking forward to the next day and the one after that.

The smell of gun oil filled the air of his office where the posse arms were kept under lock and key in an old wooden cabinet on the wall. He would miss that smell as it lingered with the tobacco smoke and fresh ink that always hung heavily in the air of the building. He would miss the badge too. Not because of the thing as a symbol, but because to him it was more like a key to helping folks. When people were at their lowest points in their lives, they relied upon the man with that badge to offer them counsel and more often than not, they listened because of the badge. He'd helped so many folks and done so much that he was proud of, but the time had come to hang it up and tend to his own flock.

Jacob would be leaving home soon. He'd even met a girl already and when he'd introduced them on the square the day before, the Sheriff could see that she was something very special to his son. The boy might not even know it yet, but it was clear to his father that he was in love.

Soon after Jacob, Sol would follow his own trail and leave them. Gaylord would be left alone then with a wife he had almost estranged over the years and a son that he didn't really know yet. But fate had given him another shot at it. He would get it right this time. Closing his eyes, Gaylord inhaled the smell of the courthouse one last time, finished his coffee and blew out the lantern just in time for the breaking of the dawn on a new day.

Staggering pie eyed from fatigue toward the door, he remembered his guns that he had hung on the hat rack behind his desk. He turned and looked at them hanging there through the dark room. "You've made it," he whispered to himself. "The

Fourth is over. Rest easy old man and get used to the weight of your walk without the irons."

Closing the courthouse door behind him, Gaylord looked up at the early morning sky in time to see a falling star as it sailed across the horizon. He paused for a moment and was grateful for another beautiful morning. Fate, he thought, was not such a bad thing after all.

As he staggered home to sleep away most of the day, the sheriff had no way of knowing that fate had not so easily forgotten him. For even as he stood staring in awe at the early morning sky and the miracles it beheld, Hiram Wilson was saddling his horse and drawing nearer him. Even as the sheriff was celebrating and giving thanks, fate was closing the gap between them like two trains running headlong toward one another on a single stretch of track.

While Gaylord Lyman finally removed his clothes and crawled into the warm bed beside his still sleeping wife and rested, Hiram Wilson rode.

Chapter 30   Chariton Morning

July 6th, 1870

Sheriff Lyman rose from his bed a little later that morning. He had done little the day before on account of having come in so late and he had plenty to do. There was little time for talks or even coffee. In fact, he even left the house without seeing anyone at all and walked out into the early morning rays of sun shining into his sleep filled eyes.

The sky was cast in orange hues that morning with streaks of shades of red and violet radiating outward into the darkness above. The Indians he had known along the Missouri would have called it a bad omen sky, but to him, it was only a pretty one to look at. There could be no bad omens on such a day, being well rested and having his last Independence Day as sheriff well in his wake.

His intentions had been to walk directly to the office that morning, but intentions are often wrought with peril by chance and circumstance and such was to be the case on that morning for Gaylord Lyman.

It seemed that the entire town was stirring already that morning, and everyone who he passed along the way came to their fence to talk with him. He had been scarce for the most part the day before, so it was the cause of every soul he encountered to tell him all about their celebrations and who had visited and what they had done. At first, he had been mildly irritated by the distractions, but as his walk advanced slowly into the morning, he gave in to the theme of day, relaxing and enjoying the conversations.

After only a few blocks into Chariton proper, Gaylord formally resigned himself to defeat of his earlier intentions of working and accepted an invitation into one of the dwellings for a cup of coffee. Following the old man up his walk, the Sheriff looked up at the roof of the tidy little home and admired the chimney. He must caulk it anew each summer, he'd thought to himself. Just that very moment, Gaylord resolved to shirk his official duties that afternoon and finally repair his own chimney.

The bricks were beginning to fall about it already and he'd been promising his wife to fix it for more than one summer. Yes, Gaylord thought to himself happily, today I shall finally fix it, by God! It was yet another way of slowly easing himself into the role of a retired sheriff. He would begin right then, slowly spending more and more time tending to his own affairs and less and less time to the affairs of the county proper. A loaded train does not stop upon a dime, he'd thought to himself. It must ease into the station for a good long while to hit its mark at the platform, and so too shall I, beginning on this very day, he thought.

A few blocks away, Evelyn and Clara stepped out the door of the Harris Inn. They spoke quietly and giggled about some man who, while passing, had stared at them until he stumbled upon a loose board along the walk. In the short time the family had stayed there, the two had become an inseparable pair. Along the Chariton Square, every boy and man who saw them coming would wait in eager anticipation to tip their hat to the beauties. Their appearance and warm, genuine smiles were more than enough to brighten most anyone's day.

As the two walked, they talked of simple things mostly, but also of the importance of the business of the day. In only a few more sunrises, Evelyn would be married to Jasper Logan and it was the business of the day to have their dresses fitted. There were also countless other arrangements that needed to be made by the two as well. There were many decisions to be made and a great deal of shopping to be done. It all gave an air of importance and excitement for the girls' day out together.

Clara was supposed to be leaving with her parents shortly after the wedding, but she was beginning to seriously question whether she could part herself from both Evelyn *and* Jacob. The loss of either one of them in her life just then would be unimaginable. But to lose both of them, at once, would most certainly prove fatal. She simply couldn't do it. The only thing that still troubled her about the decision was how best to broach it with her father.

If Jacob would ask her hand so soon, her father might refuse it for being too rash. If he waited, she may be forced to leave him behind. If she begged to stay, her father may refuse to allow it simply because of his obvious displeasure of Mr. Logan. There was much to consider that morning, but still she managed to keep a light heart and talk of simple things with her sister. It was, after all, Evelyn's moment, and Clara would not detract from it by burdening her sister with problems that were solely her own.

As the girls entered a shop on the south side of the Chariton square, a commotion rang out and their hearts skipped a collective beat as people gasped and ran. Turning about, they followed the men with their eyes who were running into the busy street. It was a courier's wagon full of barrels that had given way when a wheel had busted. Seeing that the driver was shaken but uninjured, they turned back to their business and went into the shop. What a day it was turning out to be.

Not far from them, somewhere in the Lucas County countryside, Hiram Wilson was asking a farmer for directions to Chariton.

Chapter 31   Trail's End

Hiram Wilson had no way of knowing if Clara would still be in Chariton. Her letter had arrived too late, it would seem, and the journey took him much longer than he had anticipated upon the back of the aging horse. Still, there was nothing that could come between his effort to find his one true love in this world; his only opportunity at happiness in this lifetime.

Indeed, if his father was dead as he suspected, Clara may be his only chance at happiness *ever*. Certainly, the flames of hell lapped at the soul of anyone who would strike down one of their own, he surmised. He figured that if ever, anyone would be damned for all eternity, that it would be such a man as that. Clara, it seemed, was his only opportunity to find any peace, any happiness, any sort of salvation. He had ridden for days and sometimes nights. He had been lost and starving and almost dead from thirst along the way, but still he had rode to her. It was the only thing that he *could* do, whether she remained in the town or not. If there was any sort of chance at finding her, no matter how small, he had to take it.

As Hiram rode into the edge of Chariton, he felt the eyes of every citizen upon him as he passed. He knew then that he must look a fright after so many days on the road. Through the dust and the mud and having slept in fields and riverbeds, it donned on him with the stares just how awful he had to look. Who could blame them for staring at him so?

What if Clara was still there and he rode up looking like that? What then? Would she really go with him in such a state? Certainly she wouldn't. He could never expect her to. He knew that he would simply have to take the time to clean himself, to shave, and to at the very least buy a new shirt. But buy it with what? He hadn't a penny to his name.

As the old horse trudged along the road, Hiram stopped her and realized what he must do. He would sell the horse and get enough money from the sale of it to pay their way for a spell until he found work. They could take a stage to anywhere with a few dollars and she, at least, would never have to live the sort of rugged existence that he had just endured. Climbing off of the horse, not far from the square, he began to inquire if anyone might be interested in buying the animal.

Most people only continued to look at the dirty faced, ragged stranger and turned their backs when he approached them, leading a horse in tow. He was young and skinny and dirty faced and had the accent of a Missourian to boot. It was plain for most folks to see that the horse must be stolen. Why else would a man from the south ride into town and desire to sell his only means of transport? He was clearly not aiming to settle down there.

After an hour of stopping nearly everyone he met, Hiram was becoming distraught and desperate when he happened upon Captain Robison, out for a morning stroll. The Captain, having served in the great war and having been no stranger to many a muddy trail ride himself, was less put off by the appearance of the young man than the others had been.

"Excuse me sir," Hiram said as he neared. "Would you know of anyone interested in purchasing themselves a horse?"

"Perhaps," the Captain said. The Captain as it were, was among the local horse traders and saw in the desperation of the young man's face an opportunity for profit. "Is this the animal?"

"Yes sir," Hiram replied as he stepped back beside the horse so the man could inspect him.

Captain Robison knew well the flesh of horses and he began his inspection at the teeth to age the animal before moving to look at every other aspect.

"I have ridden this animal from Missouri just now and back home it was no stranger to the plow either," Hiram said, hoping to sweeten the deal with the extra information.

"And how much did you want for it?" The Captain asked, still inspecting the hind feet.

"A hundred, twenty," Hiram replied, "and that is a steal at such a price."

Captain Robison looked him in the eyes and stood erect from the hind hooves. It was a sound animal getting along in the years, but with many more to come yet, with proper care. It would have been worth the money at that price, but the boy's eyes were tired, his physique was gaunt, and being a former Army Officer, Captain Robison knew the state of men even better than the flesh of horses.

"I'll give you forty dollars," he replied, "cash money."

Hiram was outraged by the offer. "She is worth four times as much!" he protested.

"Very well then," the old Captain said, and strolled on down the wood planking of the walk.

"Wait!" Hiram called after him.

With the sound of the word, the Captain knew that the hook had been set. Now he need only land this hungry fish and the day would be a very profitable one indeed.

"Make it eighty," the boy called after him.

The Captain smirked a bit, feeling the hook set well and he turned about slowly, trying his best to act disinterested.

"I have fifty dollars on my person," he replied as he walked back toward the pair. "I can offer you only fifty dollars."

"It is not enough, sir," Hiram replied. "I need more out of it. It is all that I have and..."

"I can give you fifty dollars," the Captain said, eyeing his quarry carefully, "and this watch. It is very dear to me too." The Captain was lying. The watch was silver and had been found upon the field of a battle by a soldier. He had won the thing in a card game along his journeys and carried it as his daily time piece, saving the gold one for better occasions.

Hiram stared down at the watch and the fifty dollar bill. Daylight was burning as he pondered the offer and he knew that Clara may well be fading from his grasp with each moment he dithered. "Sold," Hiram replied and put the money and the watch in his pocket.

Turning back to the old horse, he thanked the animal with a few strokes before reaching down to unhitch the saddle.

"The saddle goes with the horse," the Captain said plainly.

"That was not in the deal!" Hiram replied angrily, knowing the saddle had nearly as much value as the rest of the trade.

"Very well then," the Captain said. "Give me the money back."

"I will not," Hiram replied.

"Then I shall call fore the Sheriff and let him see to it," the Captain scoffed.

Hiram knew he had been beaten. He was desperate and both of them knew it. It was no position to make a good trade, being desperate and all. But there it was. He had fifty dollars in his pocket and that was enough to get them started at least. Without it, he had nothing but an old horse, filthy clothes, and an empty stomach. Hiram sighed.

"Let me get my things from the bags," he said quietly. He did not even want to look at the sparkle in the man's eye. He knew he'd been had, but he could not look to see the victorious smiling eyes of the man who had done him in. He didn't have to look anyhow. He felt them smiling at him.

Reaching in the bags, Hiram drew out the two bottles of whiskey. It was store bought and could be traded for something along the way. To his surprise, in the bottom of the other bag, his father's navy revolver sat under a small bundle of rope. If he'd known it was there he may well have been able to kill something along the way to eat. He stuffed the revolver under his belt and pulled his dirty shirt down over it.

"Any chance you'd like to sell that pistol too, boy?" The Captain asked.

"Hmmmmfff," Hiram scoffed, and turned away from the thief without another word. He had just been robbed and both of them knew it. If he had thought that the pistol was loaded for sure, he might even be tempted to turn about and shoot the man for horse thievery. Hiram half smiled at the thought of it but only walked on toward the square a few blocks away, but well within his sight. On the street behind him, Captain Robison bragged to a friend about his good fortune.

Chapter 32   Fate

Evelyn stood as a Paris statue, striking a pose of poised magnificence and voluptuous splendor while Clara looked on and the woman placed pins along the dress seam, following the contours of the young woman's body.

"What do you think?" Evelyn asked her sister. "Does it cause my hips to look too small?"

"I think it is incredible," Clara replied. "You will be the most beautiful bride in the history of Lucas County," she said, looking on in awe as the dress formed around her sister's perfect figure.

Even as the woman knelt and pinned, they heard the bells clang in the front of the store. Clara had no way of knowing that the voice of the man, muffled through the interior wall, was that of Hiram Wilson. If she had known she might have panicked. She may have fainted. She may even have hid or run out the back. But she could not have known that it was Hiram, separated from her by only a few feet and thin facade wall constructed only to offer privacy to those fortunate souls genteel enough to be purchasing fitted clothing.

A few feet between the two, and a thin wall were all that stood in the way of a fate of their own. A step by either, a slightly elevated voice to be recognized, the opening of the swinging door, and they would be face to face.

"I will have one of them shirts and a pair of the heavier trousers there," Hiram had said to the man at the counter.

The tailor looked at him suspiciously and wondered if he might try to grab the items and dash out the front door. Such things were rare occurrences to be sure, but they happened from time and time, and when they did, it was always at the hand of some dirty drifter such as the boy who stood before him.

"That will cost you a dollar and a half," the tailor said, not moving to retrieve the items, "and an extra fifteen cents to have them fitted."

Hiram reached into his pocket and pulled out the large bills he had only recently received from the exchange of his horse.

"I'll not need them fitted," he said to the tailor. "Just make the pants a little big and I will snug them with my belt."

"Suit yourself," the tailor replied, finally retrieving the items after tallying the purchase.

As if on cue, the back door swung open and the woman walked out to inform the tailor that they were ready for him. Her only duty at the shop was to tend to women customers until they were covered enough for the man to do his work. The final tailoring was very much the work of a skilled hand,

and only men could be entrusted with such knowledge at the time.

Following behind her closely, Clara slipped around the corner to admire some of the dresses in the front of the store. As she rounded the corner, she caught a glimpse of a man as he walked out, just a glimpse. The dirty stranger disappeared quickly and Clara went about admiring the fine linens and dresses of every sort.

As Hiram crossed the corner of the square through the mud, he would never know how cruelly he had been betrayed by the mysterious hands of fate. Who among us ever knows of such things? The person or event that is capable of changing our lives forever may cross our paths a hundred times within a whisker of us and we never even know of it.

Almost happily ignorant of it all, Hiram crossed to the east side of the Chariton square. In the rear of the building furthest at the south end, a small wooden sign hung precariously above a door that read, 'Saloon, Hot Bath 5 Cents', in hand painted yellow letters. Looking at his new clothes and the filthy hand that gripped them, he walked alongside the building toward the door.

There was no front door of the establishment in sight; only a dark, cave-like entrance that appeared ominous and foreboding from the sunlight of the street. Nervously, Hiram ducked his head and stepped inside. The small one room establishment was little more than a short bar and two small tables, one just large enough so that four men could squeeze around it to play cards. On this day they all were empty.

At the bar a tall skinny man turned and looked at Hiram as he walked forward. The man gave a bit of snort through his nose as if to show a basic contempt for the younger man and turned his attention back to his glass of whiskey. As the back door swung open, both of them looked away as the rays of sun shone brightly inside and the figure of a large man appeared.

The tall, fat man wore an apron that was about three sizes too small for his body and looked as if it had belonged to the man's wife perhaps. The large man stopped as he neared the bar and looked at Hiram, trying to figure if he had ever seen him there before. He hadn't, and after sizing him up, he figured him for a beggar.

"Can I help you mister?" the large man asked in a deep, surly voice.

"The sign says 'hot baths'," Hiram replied.

"That's right," the man replied. "You got money?"

Hiram reached into his pocket and flashed the man a glance of his wad. The large man smiled an almost toothless grin and shook his head in affirmation. "I'll go heat the water," he said. "Anything else?"

Hiram thought about it and felt his stomach, sick with emptiness and bile, turn inside out once more. "Can I get a steak here?"

"No," the big man replied, "but I can go and get you one next door to eat while I heat the water. I'll only charge you an extra nickel for the trouble too."

"That will do," Hiram replied, and setting his package on one of the tables, he let his tired body sink into a chair.

Sometime while the men had negotiated, the tall skinny man had slipped out the front door and disappeared, leaving Hiram alone in the unattended saloon. He had never been inside of saloon before, but he'd waited outside of them on more than one occasion while his father sat inside. Looking around he could not help but wonder why men sought to spend so much of their lives and fortunes in such a place.

The bar was only long enough for four men to stand at, shoulder to shoulder. Behind it there were three mostly empty shelves, each one with only a bottle or two on them. That reminded Hiram that in his bedroll, he still had the two flat whiskey bottles. He reminded himself to try and sell them to the man when it came time to settle up and looking around the dark, empty room, he drifted into sleep.

Chapter 33   Contact

Sheriff Gaylord Lyman was finally making his way across the town square toward the courthouse that morning, eyeing the widening crack that ran up the east side of the building. He had noticed it from a distance, but closer, now, in the street, he could see that his eyes had not deceived him. The crack in the masonry was growing with each passing day, sign of the folly of building a heavy brick structure atop wooden foundations. How much longer the building might last was only a question of how much money the county would be willing to invest in it.

He was still shaking his head at the failing design when Mr. Fallon came running up to him out of breath.

"Sheriff Lyman," Fallon called after him. The sheriff winced privately at the sound of his voice. Mr. Fallon was *always* reporting someone or something. He was do-gooder of the rare sort that the Sheriff would be glad to rid himself of.

"Good morning, Mr. Fallon," the Sheriff replied, hoping that it was only a social visit that the man had hailed him for, and not something intent upon ruining his otherwise lofty mood.

"I believe we have a horse thief in our midst," Mr. Fallon reported dutifully.

"Oh, and how come that is?" Gaylord asked suspiciously.

"The Captain has bought a horse from the ruffian not long ago," he replied. "And the dirty vile wretch rode into town on only the one and sporting a Missouri accent!"

Mr. Fallon was a member of the troublesome Anti Horse Thief Society and the sheriff knew that he had best investigate before they took it upon themselves to do so.

"I will see into it," the Sheriff replied solemnly.

"I will tell the others and prepare to ride after him if need be," Mr. Fallon replied before turning away in a half run.

"That won't be necessary, Mr. Fallon," Sheriff Lyman called after him, but the man ignored his call and continued his jog in the direction of Logan's Creamery. "Damn it," the Sheriff said softly. "God damn it all to Hell," he followed underneath his breath.

As if on cue, the tall skinny man from the bar stepped in front of the sheriff and offered a report of the dirty faced young ruffian who showed up at Clyde's Saloon with a pocket chocked full of bills.

Sheriff Lyman stood at the gate leading to the courthouse. Inside, his guns hung upon the hall tree where he had left them the prior morning. He paused momentarily and thought about retrieving them first, but knew that the Anti Horse Thief

Society men would be close behind him even if he went straight to the saloon.

"Damn it," he whispered again and he turned to follow the picketed fence to the east as it surrounded the courtyard, protecting the grasses from wandering stock. Men waved at the Sheriff and hailed him good morning as he crossed the mud road and walked steadily down along the east side of the square. He waved curtly back at them but carried on without a word, intent on beating the vigilantes to the Missourian inside the saloon.

Passing the store at the Southeast end of the square, Sheriff Lyman walked to the east along the building to the small wooden sign that read 'Saloon' above the door. It was as unsavory a place as the town had in it and he wondered why they even continued to rent the tiny little box out to old Clyde. Certainly, he was the cause of more rat infestations and fire hazards than his rent could possibly make good for.

The sheriff stepped inside and as his eyes adjusted to the light he found a young Hiram Wilson asleep in the chair. "Wake up, son," he said firmly, but quietly, recognizing the youth in the boy's face behind the mask of dirt and grime.

Hiram Wilson startled awake and sat up in his seat, staring blankly at the Sheriff.

"Yes sir?" Hiram asked the man standing opposite the table from him.

"I am Sheriff Lyman," he said. "I have some questions I would like to ask of you."

"What is it? Have I done something wrong, sir?" Hiram asked sheepishly, wondering if they hadn't discovered his father's body in Missouri and got word there somehow. Hiram swallowed hard and felt his heart begin to beat in his chest.

"No, son," the Sheriff replied. "You've done nothing wrong. It's only that I have got to ask you a few questions about the horse and..."

"What is it?" he asked.

"Look," the Sheriff replied impatiently. "There are men coming here to see about you. Let's you and me take a walk over to the courthouse. It will be safer there."

"But I have a steak and a bath coming," Hiram replied.

"It will be here for you when we're through," Sheriff Lyman replied, and hearing the sound of men coming, he reached down and grabbed Hiram by the arm. "Let's go," he said, pulling him from his seat.

Hiram had no way of knowing that men were coming for him just then. He didn't know that the Sheriff's apparent hostility was only in anticipation of the arrival of his fellow towns people. Hiram only knew that he was being pulled to his feet and then pushed out the front door of the saloon into the bright light of the Chariton summer sun.

Hiram paused, as did Sheriff Lyman, as his eyes adjusted to the blinding light once again. As they did, he looked across the street to the south and west of him and saw her. It was her. Clara stood on the corner of the street with a woman who could be her twin. She was even more beautiful and elegant than he had remembered her and Hiram desperately wished that he had changed his clothes at least or bathed.

She had yet to look across and see him yet, but Hiram stood motionless, speechless, and taken aback at finally taking in the object of so much of his affection. His heart beat hard within his breast and he could only look at her, breathless. Sheriff Lyman, hearing the sound of men's voices approaching from the alley, gave Hiram a push toward the courthouse and grabbed hold of his shirt. He was growing ever impatient with the situation and desired merely to put the thing to bed as soon as he could.

Just then, at the sight of the commotion, Clara looked up at the men. Hiram could see the strange look in her eyes and watched her lips mouth his name. "Hiram," she had said so quietly that even Evelyn could not hear it as it passed her tender lips.

"No!" Hiram screamed as the Sheriff threatened to pull him away from the one thing he held dear in the world. He pushed the Sheriff away from him and spun around brandishing his father's pistol. For a second, Hiram felt the victory of having freed himself, only to suddenly realize how much more dire he had just made his situation.

Hiram looked across the street at Clara, desperately struggling to make sense of the moment and figure some way to get them both out of that terrible place in time. The world seemed frozen within its' current state, unmoving, unchanging. Hiram had never felt so helpless in all of his life.

Sheriff Lyman grimaced. He could hear the men closing in upon the corner then. He knew that any second they would round the bend and seeing the boy brandishing a pistol, they would shoot him down as sure as the day he was born. The young man was dead and he didn't even know it.

Sheriff Lyman had ridden with hard men before. He'd arrested a good many of them too. This young boy was no hard man. There was an apparent softness about him that the experienced eye of the Sheriff could see, even behind the dirt

221

and the gun. He knew the boy had no intention of firing the pistol. And he knew by the way he held it that he had probably never even shot the thing.

But still, there was no time for talking. The sheriff stepped forward with a certainty that the boy was bluffing and demanded the gun, the way a mother demands hidden candy from her own child. Hiram was still looking at Clara and turned in just time enough to look Sheriff Lyman in the eye as the gun fired.

The men stood inches apart and stared into one another's eyes for a second that might have been an hour or a week or a lifetime. Sheriff Lyman, feeling his belly and realizing the location and size of the wound, knew what the boy had done.

"You have killed me," he said to Hiram, their eyes fixed.

Hiram could only look at him in horror, wondering how it had come to that. Turning, he looked at Clara once again and ran to a nearby horse, freeing it from the tie near the alley and riding swiftly away toward the wooded lot just east of town.

"Oh Lord," Sheriff Lyman called out, holding his wound and feeling innards trying to push out of the gaping hole in his belly. "He has killed me!" he said, slumping to his knees from the shock that threatened to take him even before the bullet finished its work.

As the crowd gathered around the Sheriff and men ran to fetch doctors, some others rode up to report on the direction of the flight of the fugitive. In minutes, the bulk of the men who called themselves The Anti Horse Theft Society had assembled, and rode out after the fugitive with Jasper Logan leading the way.

Chapter 34   Caught

If Hiram had been thinking, he would have kept riding on that horse as fast as he could, as far away from Chariton as he could get. If he'd had his wits about him just that second, he would have gone through those woods without stopping and kept going until he hit the river, any river, then floated as far downstream as the current would carry him away from Lucas County to another state, another country even. But as he rode out of Chariton, Hiram had not been thinking so clearly. Instead, he had turned back once and looked at *her* again. Clara, he thought, is right there. I can still have her, he'd believed. He had looked her in the eyes and saw her mouth his name. She was waiting him for him still, he'd believed.

When he reached the wooded grove at the edge of Chariton, Hiram leapt from the horse and swatted it away. He had hoped that it would keep riding away and the men would follow it. He had thought in that instant that he could hide in the woods until dark and then sneak into town and get Clara. He had thought it so for only an instant, but when the horse only galloped a few dozen yards into the clearing and stopped, he knew that all had been lost.

Running deeper into the woods, he heard the men screaming. Crossing a small ditch, he heard them holler back and forth as they found the horse. If only he'd stolen a younger, wilder horse, he'd thought. Or if only he'd ridden 'round the woods at least instead of stopping right there, he might have had a chance, even a small one. As men began to enter the woods above him, Hiram could only hunker down in a heavy brush pile and conceal himself with leaves and dirt and anything he could collect within his reach, and pray that they might not see him.

As the voices drew nearer, Hiram held his breath and tried to stop his body from shaking. He feared that even the beating of his heart would betray him to the men as they closed in on him. Looking up from within his brushy tomb, Hiram almost yelped aloud when he realized that there, standing directly above him was a horse, with a man atop it scanning the horizon. He thought for a second that he might shoot him, or knock him off with a branch and steal the horse to get away, but as the horse stepped forward, he was relieved to have missed the opportunity.

Instead, he only lay there in the dirt and the brush with sticks and thorns poking him in the side of his back. As the minutes ticked slowly past the voices grew further and further away from him and he thought that he might have slipped through their net at last. At first, he checked the watch every so often to pass the time, but as he found the minutes passed too slowly for his liking he ceased to look at the thing. He had shot the sheriff at around eleven o'clock, and the last time he would look at the watch it read three o' clock. If he could only hold out in such a way a little longer and not be discovered, then all may not be lost. He forgot about his ill conceived plan to go into town. But still, he thought, Clara would certainly come to look for him after dark. She would have to know that he would not have gone far without her. If only he could last until dark, he'd thought.

As he lay there dreaming of her calling his name out into the night air, he heard the sound of men once again growing steadily closer. He lay there, trying to think himself part of the landscape as the voices drew near. There were more of them now, he thought. Every muscle in his body tensed in fear as the footsteps crunched twigs on the forest floor. Hiram closed his eyes tightly, fearing that even the whites of his eyes might give him away. As the footsteps were all about him, he heard a set of them stop, and for a moment he imagined himself riding across an open prairie somewhere near his home with Clara on the stallion behind him, holding him tightly.

Click. The sound of the pistol cocking beside his ear was unmistakable. Hiram opened his eyes and sat up with his own pistol pointed at the man. "Keep still," Hiram whispered to him as he drew himself to his knee.

Hiram finally had a good look at the woods about him. There was a solid line of men in each direction. As he tried to pull himself to his feet, he knew he'd been caught, but his body was as stiff from rigor as a day's dead animal. He stretched himself to stand and as he did, his own pistol fired into the air, just missing the head of the man. The man barely startled, but looked at Hiram in disbelief. Instead of shooting him where he sat, the man raised his pistol and clubbed him atop the head. Hiram fell back to the ground and in an instant, everything went black.

As he came to in a start, the men held firm grips upon each arm and a larger group of men assembled around him. They cursed and spat upon him until the tall, gangly man he'd first seen at the saloon that morning appeared in front of him, peered in his eyes, and produced a rope and a smile.

225

"Hang him!" the man announced, followed by others of the same mind. Hiram could feel the tension building when a man ran up to the group and announced that the Sheriff was alive and wanted to see the shooter. The men grudgingly accepted the desire of the injured sheriff, and only took turns among them walking him out of the woods and dolling out beatings and insults.

As they walked through the streets of the town, Hiram scanned the faces of the crowd for Clara. He only wanted to see her face once more. His mind had still not wrapped itself around the seriousness of the situation. It was almost too much for him to take in. Perhaps on another day, he'd have understood it all more clearly. But on this day, he could only think of *her* still. Somehow, it seemed, that with her so close to him, that everything would work itself out. *Somehow.*

He never did see her face as he walked. There were only the scores of angry men and women taking turns to stare at him, or curse, or even run in close enough to spit in his face.

On the courthouse lawn, even more men had assembled waiting to see the scoundrel with their own eyes. It did not take much studying on behalf of any of them to see that the man was everything they thought he would be. Hiram Wilson was exactly what they expected with his grubby appearance, his shoddy clothing, his grime covered face, burn scarred on one side. If he'd only had the bath or put on the new shirt, anything to have made him look more like one of them, things may have been different. But his tired eyes and dirty presence and the hungry gauntness of his sunken cheeks were the picture of some half crazed Missouri bandit that so many of them had in their minds.

It was *this* Hiram Wilson that the people of the town gathered around and it was *this* Hiram Wilson that voices went out all about him, to hang.

A different man, brandishing a different rope stepped forward and as the men closed in around him, yet another man appeared and as if through divine providence, he reiterated the sentiments of Sheriff Lyman to have words with his assailant. Once more, the sheriff managed to save him from the throng, and Hiram was led away by a small group of men toward the building that housed a wounded Gaylord Lyman.

Inside, the Sheriff lay surrounded by doctors and people rushed in and out as if in some hurry to procure this or that, or *someone* with the ability to help the situation. Hiram was led into a room by two of the men and another followed behind him with a gun stuck into his back. Sheriff Gaylord Lyman lay upon a bed and as he heard the commotion enter the room, he pushed aside one of the doctors to see the young man.

He shook his head as if he were greeting an old friend.

"Please forgive me," Hiram cried, tears running down his cheeks as he looked at the bloodstained bandages wrapping the man's midsection. Seeing him lying there gasping for air, he realized for the first time what he had truly done. Even as the Sheriff spoke, his labored breathing revealed the last words of a dying man. Hiram had seen enough death upon the farm to know when it was coming. It was all he could do to stand as his knees weakened and his stomach churned.

The aging Sheriff had already found his own peace with death. He'd known when the gun went off that it was fate come calling for him. He'd borrowed on days that he had not earned and wasted them, every one. He even found humor in himself, that he had been foolish enough to think he had outrun his fate on the prairie and that he could keep on ignoring it forever. He was sad, sure enough, at it arriving when he had finally set his mind to doing right by it. But still, there it was.

He should've died out on that prairie so many years before, he'd thought. Those damned Indians had just kept right on following him and finally, they had caught up to him. He held no more blame against the young man who had pulled the trigger than you can blame a cat who kills a mouse. It was simply as it was meant to be.

"I forgive you, son," he'd said, feeling sorry for the younger man. He knew that he would not be well enough to protect him and see that he was delivered justice properly. He wouldn't be there to tell them that he knew it was an accident and beg for the young man's life. He tried to tell them even then, but he knew that the buffoons of The Anti Horse Thief Society would pay no mind to his words as he lay there dying. "I forgive you," he said sadly.

Hiram Wilson could only look at the man and cry. "I'm sorry." He said. "I am so sorry," and with that the men dragged him back out of the room, the doctors insisting on getting back in close to have their way with the dying man.

As they crossed the courthouse lawn once again, more and more men had gathered. Once again the cry went out to hang him and another man stepped up with a rope he had readied for the occasion. "Hang him!" they screamed aloud. "Hang him!" The cry continued as the growing throng of men milled about the courthouse lawn.

Among them were the prominent men of the town. A banker, a lawyer, a lumberyard owner, *a creamery owner*, and even a preacher were set upon hanging this heathen from Missouri and sending him back to the depths of hell from whence he had ridden. Anyone saying that the shooting was an accident was dismissed and nothing could pass for sense among the building tension within the crowd.

One of the few men who had spoken to the Sheriff and knew well his wishes was his deputy. and with his gun drawn, he grabbed Hiram by the arm and walked backwards toward the courthouse doors while others argued about the fate of the prisoner, the merit of the law, and the cost of a trial. It took only a few seconds of the crowd turning against itself in argument and the deputy slipped Hiram inside of the courthouse and secured him inside a cell. Behind him, the U.S. Marshall secured the door crossways with a wooden beam and both men settled in for what looked to be a very long night.

Chapter 35   Confessions

Like the rest of the citizens who had been out that morning on the Chariton square, Evelyn had turned and run at the sound of a shot ringing out. Clara however, could only stand and watch the two men face each other, frozen in time. She saw the look of horror on Hiram's face, and she could see the crimson red blood spot on Sheriff Lyman's abdomen slowly spread across the front of his shirt. Only when Evelyn had run back and grabbed her sister's arm, had Clara been pulled from the nightmare as it unfolded before her eyes.

By the time they had reached the safety of the tailor shop doorway, Clara had turned just in time to watch as Hiram Wilson stole a horse and headed for the outskirts of Chariton to the east. She watched out the window as men climbed swiftly upon their horses to chase out after him. And she could hear well the screams of Sheriff Lyman as he fell to the ground where he stood, clutching his stomach.

Finally, as the girls emerged from the shop, she even watched as the Sheriff was carried into a local shop. And, as they stood there upon the boardwalk while Evelyn exchanged stories of the ordeal with other witnesses, Clara watched as Jacob Lyman ran with all of his might to the store where his father lay dying. Even as the world blurred and spun around her, Clara could only stand in quiet horror at what she was feeling inside. She never said a word, or gave a whimper, but only succumbed to the moment and collapsed unconscious on to the boardwalk.

When Clara came to, Evelyn and several other women stood over her, looking down and dabbing her forehead with a wet cloth.

"Hiram," she said quietly as she opened her eyes.

"He is not here, Clara," Evelyn replied. "You have fainted I am afraid. And no small wonder, given what you've witnessed today."

"No," Clara said angrily as she sat up, clutching her sister by the arms firmly. "It was Hiram."

"What?" Evelyn looked confused for a moment, then her eyes widened as she finally understood, "The man who shot Sheriff Lyman?"

"Yes," Clara said, and began to sob uncontrollably.

"We must go then," Evelyn said, bringing her sister to her feet.

The girls marched to the shop where they had seen Sheriff Lyman carried. Inside there were a growing number of people. Some rushed to and fro with linens and pails of water. Others merely stood off to the side in disbelief and watched the scene unfold around them.

Jacob Lyman looked up from his stool beside his father. His eyes immediately found Clara through the crowd. He bolted from his seat and shielded Clara's view of his wounded father. It was no sight for a young woman's eyes.

Seeing her weep was more than Jacob could take. He grabbed her and held her tightly in his arms.

"Shhhh," he whispered to her. "It will be alright my love. He is at peace with the thing."

"Oh Jacob," she wailed quietly, "I am so sorry."

Jacob turned and walked the couple outside behind the business. Evelyn had already joined in with the growing number of women preparing linens and water and cleansing the blood soiled ones.

"I'm so sorry," Clara said again, in the quiet of the alley porch behind the shop.

"You needn't fret love," he reassured her. "Every doctor in town is seeing to him."

"It is my fault, Jacob," she said through her tears.

"That is ridiculous, Clara," he said curtly. "Stop talking so. You did nothing..."

"It was Hiram!" she exclaimed, "The boy who came for me. It was he who shot your father, Jacob!"

He stepped back away from her, mouth agape and looked confused and bewildered. For a moment he thought to push her from him and turn away from her forever. But through her tears and sadness and weeping, he looked into her eyes and knew that she was still the girl he loved. She was still as an angel from the heavens above, and whatever else she may be, whatever trouble she might have wrought into this world to him, he could never turn his back upon her.

"It was not of your hand," he said quietly, pulling her back into the reassuring safety of his arms. "Do not speak of him, or of your knowledge of it ever again, Clara," he whispered.

"Oh Jacob," she wailed.

"Look at me," he said, raising her chin with his finger softly until her eyes met his own. "You had no hand in this, Clara. Now promise me on your own father that you will never speak of this again. There are many who would think ill of you for it and I will have none of it. Not on the day of my own father's death. Now promise me, Clara."

"I promise, Jacob," she said, drawing in her breath to regain some small form of composure.

"Good," he said. "Now I need to be in there with him. You go to the Inn and I will come for you when this thing is over."

"Alright, Jacob," she said. "But I just...I am so..."

"Shhhh," he said, "remember always your promise to me."

"Jacob," she said as he turned to go back into the building where his father lay dying.

"Yes?" he stood in the doorway and looked solemnly at her.

"I love you," she said. "No matter what had happened today, I was yours and yours alone."

"And I you," he said, "more than anyone, more than ever. Now go, and remember your word to me." Jacob turned and disappeared into the building.

Clara looked up into the sky and felt the rays of the hot July sun glaring down upon her. She knew that with Jacob by her side, that she could conquer anything. She fed from the strength within him and felt stronger herself because of it. If he could maintain himself thus though *this* day, then by God, so too could she. She raised her head, wiped her tears and sought Evelyn to return with her to the Inn.

Only yards away from them, locked inside of the courthouse, Hiram Wilson wept.

Chapter 36   Hiram's End

The clanking of the steel cage was enough for Hiram to finally resign himself that it was over. Not his life, but rather, his hopes of ever getting away from it all with Clara. He had prayed with everything in his soul to be able to see her, to hold her in his arms, and let the warmth of her spirit wash away the bitter cold winds that blew relentlessly across the barren deserts of his soul. He had followed the ember within his heart to this, the only conclusion that he could have hoped for, he believed.

What else could have happened? Had he really believed that he was destined to walk away from so much misery and simply stumble his way through to a happy ending? The world was not such a place. His was no world for happy endings and the clanging of the black steel bars closing behind him was a stark reminder of the realities of this thing he called a life. He was nothing in this world and now, the tiny glimmer of hope for something better, anything better, faded as black as the iron cage that separated him from the only thing that could have saved him; Clara.

The cage was not much wider than a man and not much taller than a man either. It was a square cage with a bar top like you might expect to find some wild animal in at a traveling medicine show. Was that all that he was then, a wild animal? Certainly, the people of the town seemed to think so, and examining his clothes and dirty fingers, Hiram knew that he must look very much the part. It was only then that he confessed his real name to the men who served as his captors *and* protectors.

"My name is Hiram Wilson, of Missouri," he said quietly.

The deputy and marshal had been sitting, shotguns in hand, listening quietly to the ebb and flow of the mood of the crowd outside. They both looked up at him.

"And the horse?" the marshal inquired.

"It *is* stolen," Hiram replied, and said nothing more of it.

It was enough for the marshal to know that it was indeed stolen. That the young man offered no other alibis for his crimes was evidence enough for the marshal and he resolved to do little else to stop them, should the townspeople seek to hang him again. If the young man had confessed earlier to his crime, the marshal thought to himself, he'd already be swinging somewhere.

Hiram gave no further consideration to saving himself from whatever the law might deliver unto him. He knew he'd killed that sheriff, sure enough, and he suspected his own father to be lying dead in a Missouri woodshed. In the emptiness of the iron cage, and to only the sounds of men yelling at one another outside, Hiram Wilson hung his head and wept. It was over.

It is a hard thing when you learn that your life would never be what you'd hoped. It is a harder thing still to know that your hopes and dreams will never come true at all. To learn these things in an instant though, and know that not only will things not be as you had thought, but that you've no hope beyond breathing that very second...is more than any soul can endure.

In Hiram's heart, blackness settled in unlike anything he had ever known before. During every beating he had ever received, through every harsh word and every disparaging event, there had always been a dim ember of hope. Then though, standing within the confines of the cage and hearing men calling for his life, there was nothing save the darkness of despair and the harshness of hopelessness. Not even God would do for him now, and the only soul he had ever loved was beyond his reach forever.

The only thing remaining for Hiram to feel was hunger. The dull, painful grumbling within his stomach was the only thing that marked him still as a man. But did not any wild beast within a cage also feel the same? Alas, even that could not be assuaged as there was no food within the walls of the courthouse; no reprieve from his suffering; not even that.

As the church bells rang out through the town, Hiram sensed a growing uneasiness about his captors. They rose from their seats and paced, checking their weapons, peeking out windows, and whispering to one another. If there had been anything at all within Hiram's stomach, he would have purged it a hundred times that day. As it were, as the sounds of the growing crowd outside in the darkness became more enraged, Hiram tasted only the bile as it came into the back of his mouth. He tried to throw up in a corner of his cell, but there was only a little more bile, coating his dry mouth. He had not even the saliva to spit it out. The only thing left was to taste it, and feel the hungry acids burning the inside of his mouth and throat.

When the door burst open and a flood of men rushed in, the deputy and the marshal only lay down their arms in the corner of the room and raised their hands to their neighbors. It was as if the two were merely actors upon a stage and having played their own parts to the end of the charade, became mere spectators of the remainder of the drama.

Hiram had no fight left within him as the men unlocked the cage and dragged him from it. "Murderer!" one man yelled, spitting in Hiram's eye. "Assassin," screamed another as he struck Hiram in the side of the head.

The men led him only a few steps away from his cell door and stopped just outside of the courthouse. The south doors had been made a shambles, rammed clean through with a chunk of tree trunk wielded by a number of men. The makeshift battering ram had run through even the thick brace that had been placed to secure the doors.

Above him, the second story of the window of the courthouse opened and the men around him looked up. Hiram too, looked up, to see Jasper Logan with his head outside, throwing down a rope to the men below. On the ground, Logan's man, Mr. Hansen, placed the rope securely around Hiram's neck.

"Have you any last words?" Mr. Hansen asked.

Hiram felt his heart beating in his chest and knew that all was not lost. He saw the crowd pause and looked into the eyes of the faces all about him, and saw that some of them appeared to show pity. Hiram sought to appeal to these; the most human of the men about him and looked directly into the eyes of such men when he spoke.

"Gentlemen," he said, "I want you all to forgive me; I am a poor boy; my mother died when I was small. It is the first time I ever committed a crime; I was in liquor at the time."

The last part had been a lie. But, the rest were true, and had he not heard his father a thousand times claim to have been in liquor when he had done something foolish or horrible? And didn't other men seem to understand such an excuse for nearly any actions? Perhaps, these too were such men. Hiram saw some of the faces weaken slightly. He was getting through to them, he'd thought. He struggled through his desperation to find the right words to finish his plea and win his life for the moment.

"I.." Hiram said, looking a man in the eye who had more pity within him than any of the rest, but that was all he could muster as the rope tightened.

Above, in the window, Jasper Logan and another man had run the end of the rope out another window and then back in again. As they began to pull the rope, it hung up on the brickwork and even frayed, threatening to snap. Seeing it, Jasper released it again and Hiram fell back to his feet, choking. Then, having run the rope straight into the window once again, the men heaved him up and secured it to a stove leg in the middle of the room.

Below them, Hiram Wilson choked. At first, it felt as if someone had hit him in the throat with a mallet. In a few moments, the pain was nothing in comparison to the struggle to grasp a breath. The knot within the rope had been as hastily tied as the plans to execute him had been laid, and it allowed a tiny bit of air to pass through his neck at first. As it did, the bile mixed and made a gurgling noise as he struggled to suck a breath through his narrowing esophagus. In the end, it only grew narrower until even the tiny gurgle subsided and his throat swelled forever closed.

Hiram thought that his head might explode from the pressure. His entire head felt as though a blacksmith's anvil had been dropped on it. And then, finally, everything went black.

To the crowd below, almost five minutes had passed since they first drew taught the rope and the time when Hiram Wilson finally ceased to kick. A preacher, who had stood among the throng all the while, and had even called for his death, stepped forward and pronounced Hiram Wilson dead.

In the window above, Jasper Logan looked down and smiled to other men, proud of their victory and satisfied that justice had been well served. As he did so, he could not have known that across the street, along the boardwalk, on the Southside of the Chariton square, Evelyn and Clara had stood holding one another close throughout the entire ordeal. Jacob Lyman arrived behind them just in time to see Hiram Wilson's last quiver and kick.

Chapter 37   After Hiram

Two days after the death of Hiram Wilson and Sheriff Gaylord Lyman, the Smith family loaded their carriage and headed out of Chariton, bound for a fresh, new beginning in the comparative wilds of Nebraska. Clara had mourned deeply for the end of Hiram. But she had also mourned with Jacob for the loss of his father. More than anyone, it was most difficult on her and she was haunted by the event until the day she died, decades later.

As the carriage pulled out and drove through the town, people stopped to look at the most beautiful sisters who had ever graced Chariton's streets. To the surprise and dismay of Jasper Logan, Evelyn loaded her things with her family and left Lucas County, and Jasper, in her past.

Evelyn and Ellis would find another and the three of them would settle even further west in the shadow of the mountains in Wyoming. For as much as she had been affected by it all, Evelyn would be grateful mostly for what Hiram Wilson had saved her from; a life with a man she would never love, and never trust to rear her children.

Jasper, it turned out, was generally shocked at her announcement when she had called off the wedding. It was her loss after all. He'd stormed out of Mrs. Harris' Inn in a barrage of curses, which ceased only when he received a busted nose from the girls' father. Walking away, his whimpers were the last thing they would ever hear from him.

As the head of the Anti Horse Thief Society, Jasper received a description of a horse that had been recently stolen from the country west of St. Louis. With a growing number of questions brewing around the circumstances, Jasper announced that the stolen animal, and the one sold by Hiram was one and the same. Jasper bought the horse immediately, shot it and killed it, then buried it on his farm. To further ensure that no one would ever investigate the incident, he sent three hundred dollars in gold to a man in Missouri who had reported a stolen horse most similar to the one Hiram had rode into town on that day.

When Mallory and his interests went broke shortly after the new century and their banks in Chariton collapsed to runs, Jasper Logan would live to see his entire fortune lost and every interest sold. Many folks said it was a curse because of what he had done so many years before. Curse or not, the irony was not missed on Chariton's oldest citizens when Jasper placed a noose around his own neck and leaped from the walkway in the creamery building.

Sheriff Gaylord Lyman was laid to rest at the Chariton Cemetery just south of town. Hiram Wilson's body would be carried in the back of a wagon, with not so much as a box or a sheet, and buried in a shallow pauper's grave in the tattered clothes he had come to town in. He was intentionally left shallow so that anyone who cared to visit the site would smell the boy's rotting flesh not far beneath the surface of the unmarked grave.

Some months later, another poorly dressed Missourian rode into town and asked after Hiram. The old man was later reported to have been seen standing over the grave of his son weeping. When he rode away, he'd left an empty bottle of whiskey in his wake and a small stone to mark the grave of his son. Elias Wilson had come only to curse his son one final time for having ruined his good name of all things. The stone was symbol within the man's eyes that he had always done right by the boy. Shortly thereafter, the stone would be broken and removed by local residents and Hiram Wilson would fade into the realm of distant memory.

Clara Smith would live her life not far from Evelyn in the hills of Wyoming. She would have many children too and live to see even more grandchildren. She would also live to see the automobile arrive and radio and all sorts of amazing things they had never imagined in those days. She and her husband, a retired sheriff, would be married for sixty years before he would finally pass to the great beyond. After all of those years, Clara would follow her husband to death within only a few moons. Born Clara Smith in Illinois in 1851, she was buried in Wyoming in 1932.

Her grave is marked by a tall slender stone with intricate flowing angels on either side. She had asked to have it so and be buried in a plot in the valley between two of the Laramie Mountains in Wyoming. Her sister Evelyn was there on the day she was buried too, and she was the only living soul who knew the significance of it all. For in her youth, her sister had been torn almost in half between the two great loves of her life. Those loves were depicted in those angels for the entire world to finally see and even in the peaks of the mountains on either side of her.

The stone though, for all of its intricate details was simple in words. It reads succinctly enough:

Clara Lyman
Devoted Wife of Jacob
1851-1932

Epilogue

Sheriff Gaylord Lyman died on July 6th, 1870 at shortly after 10:00pm. So too, did Hiram Wilson. The newspapers, with all of their accounts and intricate knowing details of the entire sordid affair, never once gave mention of *who* had lynched Hiram Wilson. No one was ever held accountable for it and the official version of events as reported in the newspapers were left to stand.

When first I read the newspaper account of the incident, there were many things that troubled me. The more I investigated the events, the more the facts behind the story grew only more disturbing.

First it is this excerpt of the account from the Chariton newspaper:

"He had a bad look, apparently brutalized in all his nature, and betrayed but little anxiety for his situation until the final demand was made upon the officers, when he begged of them to save him, and on being told that his time had come, he

pleaded to have his shackles taken off, and that was all he asked. He was a desperate character, and would have fought like a tiger. He met his fate as he would a dinner or an ordinary business matter, and seemed, to the last, to feel that he was still worth several dead men."

This really got me to thinking. Who would know better the nature of a man and how *"brutalized in all his nature"* a man was than a sheriff in 1870? Yet, for some reason, the real Sheriff Lyman, lying in his death bed with the knowledge that he was dying sent out repeated calls to see the boy and let him know that he forgave him.

If Hiram were really such a scoundrel, why would Sheriff Lyman have been so concerned about *that* of all things? No. There must have been something in that exchange. A seasoned sheriff, in my mind, would not have flinched in fear at a twenty-one year old kid with a gun. But when the shot did ring out, they had to have looked into one another's eyes and in that moment, Sheriff Lyman saw *something* in the boy worthy of making his forgiveness a dying wish.

The next thing that I found deeply disturbing is about the citizens themselves. For as much as they were concerned about the poor sheriff and hell bent on dolling out justice, Sheriff Gaylord Lyman was laid to rest under an inexpensive stone and by all accounts, his family was left to suffer in economic despair for the loss of him.

The next troubling thing in my own mind has to do with the horse itself. After the incident, a detailed description was produced of a horse that had been from a county in far eastern Missouri. If this was indeed true, then we must believe that a 20 or 21 year old Hiram Wilson left his own town and ventured some 15 days ride via horseback to the east, stole a horse, and rode the thing some 20 days back to the northwest to sell it.

Or, in miles, Hiram left his home, some fifty or so miles southeast of Chariton, traveled 150 miles to steal a horse, then traveled another 200 or so miles to sell it; all of this in a day when the best horse *might* make 18 miles a day or so.

And who, in 1870, would ride into a strange town and sell their only horse? This was the ultimate question of why I wrote this book. In my mind, there had to be a story behind it all that answered some of these questions. In newspaper accounts, the bad man in a black hat rides into town and guns down the man in the white hat. It is all simple enough really; black and white, good and evil; right and wrong. But real life is not so neat and clean is it?

Finally, Hiram Wilson's grave was never given a marker of any kind.

I think of this often when I visit an old cemetery. Beneath every marker are buried a thousand forgotten stories; a lifetime of triumphs and tragedies, lost loves and blooming spring romances. Anyone can stop and look at the name and the dates and try to imagine what might have been. You can touch the granite, run your finger along the etched names and at least conjure in your mind's eye, the image of a lifetime. For all of the *good Christians* who graced the streets of Chariton in 1870, none were moved by the forgetting of the journey that one young man had called a life, and none could forgive as much as the one man who had been wronged most and lost his own life: Sheriff Gaylord Lyman.

Accounts of the day do vary in one detail; some say Hiram Wilson was pulled and strangled to death while others say he was thrown from the second story window. In my mind, the accounts of his statements, and all else, point to him being slowly strangled from a standing position on the ground.

247

Additional Information

Let me begin by saying that the story you have just read is a fictional one. While the newspaper accounts are real and the names of the two primary actors (Sheriff Gaylord Lyman and Hiram Wilson) have been retained for the story, all other names and characters are completely fictional. If you visit the Lyman grave for instance, you will discover that Bella was not his wife's name, and their children did not consist of only three sons. For the purpose of telling the best story that I can, I purposely do not research every actor. That would limit my ability to create compelling interactions between secondary characters.

Sheriff Gaylord Lyman lies buried in the main Chariton, Iowa Cemetery, just south of town on State Highway 14. If you cross the bridge on your way to Corydon and turn right into the main entrance of the cemetery, Sheriff Gaylord Lyman's grave can be found just inside the gates, to the right (North) of the road in the second row of markers. His wife's marker is right beside his.

Hiram Wilson lies buried in an unmarked grave at the Douglass Cemetery about a mile of South of Chariton. You can find it in 2011 by heading West from the Harley Davidson dealership, then turning south on 4th Street just before you drive across the overpass. Follow the gravel to the south (veer left) across the tracks and before you reach the sharp curves in the road there is a small sign on the right hand side of the road marking the cemetery. The cemetery was once lost to time and brush, but local residents have renewed it and it is marked by a flag and salvaged stones set in concrete. A short walk from the road and tucked behind a home, it is worth of every step of the journey.

The place where Hiram Wilson shot Sheriff Gaylord Lyman is located just outside of the furthest south building on the East side of the Chariton square. In 2011, the business inside is a coffee shop called *Get Mugged* and inside you will find some very nice ladies who will be more than happy to talk to you about Hiram Wilson, Sheriff Lyman, and all things Lucas County. With coffee in hand and a great sandwich in your belly, you can stand just outside of *Get Mugged* and see the spot where the Sheriff was gunned down, then look across to the South doors of the County Courthouse and imagine where Hiram was hanged.

The "city lake" as it was called in the day was a small natural lake. This long forgotten feature of Chariton would have been an important part of the landscape drawing early settlers to the spot. Between then and now, the water has been drained, but a deep depression in the landscape still remains today. It can be seen along the route of Highway 14 (7th Street), and is the 2011 location of what is currently referred to as Yocom Park.

The civil war cannon said to have been fired at the top of each hour is also very real. When it got in the way of construction and progress, it was simply buried beneath the Chariton square somewhere. On many occasions the city has sought to have it located, but to this day its exact location remains a mystery.

For more information about *The Lynching of Hiram Wilson* come and visit us in Lucas County, Iowa. For the most part, we are very friendly people eager to chat and quick to assist others. And, we are proud to announce that 2011 marks our 141st consecutive year of not having lynched a Missourian or any other visitors, so rest easy when you come!

For more information about Buzz Malone, please visit www.buzzmalone.com

I always enjoy hearing from readers, so please feel free to drop me an e-mail there and I will be happy to get back with you. As an independent author without the assistance of a big city agent or publisher, my success or failure depends on each and every one of you. If you enjoyed this story, please tell a friend about it. Thanks for reading.

-Buzz Malone-

More sites of interest:

http://www.charitonchamber.com/

http://www.lucascountytourism.org/

http://lucascountyhistoricalsociety.blogspot.com/

http://iagenweb.org/lucas/

http://buzzmalonebooks.blogspot.com/

The Lynching of Hiram Wilson by Buzz Malone

8420498R0

Made in the USA
Charleston, SC
07 June 2011